THE STORY OF JENNY GREENTEETH, by one who knew her

D.K. Renton

First published by Hegemon Press, 2025

ISBN: 978-1-0369-1876-7

CONTENTS

CHAPTER 1
WHO BY WATER

Niamh was watching Liam. She was practising again the speech she'd been preparing all afternoon. She was going to confront him with the cruelty of what he'd done. He'd been gossiping about her – it had to be him. She wouldn't swear. She was going to keep her voice controlled, tell the truth, watch how he reacted. He hadn't asked her permission to blab. She was going to be as precise as the woman from Newsnight. *She was.* All she needed was a way of separating Liam from Aitch and from Jake. Then, she'd confront him, not that he was listening. He was staring at his keys – at a yellow plastic clip he'd fished from his pocket. Fuck-face Liam fiddled at the clip, pulled back when it broke in half. He stood up.

"Don't mind me," he said, and he beamed a little, absent-minded smile. He walked over to the Street Fighter machine, leaving the others. She rose to follow.

"Round one," the machine sang. But she couldn't have the conversation with him, not now, not with the stupid game cossetting him. She sat back down again.

They were in a pub, the Chapel Bar, Islington. March 2013. Niamh knew she should be walking to the games console, standing beside Liam, making use of the fact that he couldn't run away. But she didn't want to look desperate. If she came over to him now, her voice would shiver. She'd have become that awful thing, the needy ex-girlfriend.

"Round two," the machine shouted in its samurai voice.

"UPPER cut." Niamh knew Liam liked to play Ryu. She'd seen how the character moved, spinning across the screen, a white blur of gleeful violence. She heard him slam a fist against the screen. "Arseholes."

The others were there too. Niamh looked at Aitch, whose real name wasn't even Aitch, it was Helen for Christ's sake. Niamh was being very polite and saying nothing about the green dungarees which made Aitch look like she was thirteen.

"Tired?" Aitch asked.

"It's not been a great day," Niamh said.

Other evenings in the Chapel Bar, she'd enjoyed the leather couches, the wooden tables, the footstools. Tonight, though, the time-capsule décor wasn't doing anything for her. Not least because Jake, who was sitting on the other side of Aitch, had claimed the footstool before Niamh could stop him. What about her needs? The shriek of the console, "FIGHT." The couches weren't helping, not when Liam had his eyes locked on the screen.

The glass was empty, but it wasn't her turn, she'd bought the last round and Aitch the one before that. The boys weren't paying their fair share.

"Hey," she'd told Jake. "Are you planning to get a round in anytime?"

"I'm doing it," he said, not even looking at her as he spoke, but at Aitch. Who was keeping her eyes fixed on Liam.

With a thump on the console, Liam returned to the friends, his eyes on his shoes. He said a rueful, "The button's stuck." He picked up his beer, downed it. "Mine's a Guinness."

"Got it," said Jake.

Niamh wanted to rage at Jake, the speed with which he sprang up to help Liam, but she couldn't make herself fume. She liked Jake. He could taste the difference between a five-pound and a twenty-pound bottle of wine. He was good with food, too. The cookbooks in his flat had pencil drawings on their covers and names like perfume bottles, *Euphoria, Mirth*. Every time they went back there after closing, Niamh ended up reading the cookbooks instead of smoking Jake's Hindu Kush. When something was on Jake's mind he talked and talked and never let it go. He kept a blog for all the books he read. Sometimes Liam read them after him. When he did, Niamh would look on eBay and read the same authors as them. "I don't know where you find the time," Aitch said, when she found out. She made it sound like there was a mystery, but there wasn't. Niamh suffered the boys' prolix favourites, *Infinite Jest*, *A Confederacy of Dunces*, trawling for the clues that might return Liam to her.

Back, Jake came with his friend's drink. "Good times."

"The best," Liam answered.

"Where's my drink," said Niamh. Then, when there was no answer, "Fuck you."

Liam and Niamh were historians, while Jake studied Aerodynamics and Aitch Earth Sciences. Liam was the one whose offer of a pint had first brought them together five months before. Even now, he was the still point around which they turned. He never had harsh words for anyone. He could always find a story to lift the mood. She liked the way he looked – his hair grade one all over, the linen jacket, the cashmere sweater. She'd loved him, until he transformed into the dick-lord who'd started the rumours which had made her life hell. How did that work, how could anyone be her saviour and her enemy, both at once?

For a week, Niamh had kept silent as Aitch attached herself to Liam's side. Three days ago, the two of them had vanished into the dark before returning with a smile on Liam's face and the third button on Aitch's shirt undone, but they hadn't gone home together afterwards. Not that their delay was any comfort to Niamh. Tonight was going to be the night, she knew it, not that Aitch would have told Liam yet. By tomorrow, they'd be a couple.

Aitch stood. "Laters," she said, and she and Liam left the pub, his fingers trapped in the net of her embrace. They walked out into the cold.

Niamh turned to Jake. "What're we going to do?"

"Us?" said Jake.

"The night's ours. We could go back to yours, get shit-faced."

"You've had three pints already."

"Or come back to mine," Niamh said, "listen to some music." She hated herself, knew how needy she sounded, but she wasn't ready to return home, not to her landlady Vron who'd be waiting up for her, ready to quiz Niamh on the scandal of her evening.

Jake said, "They've got music here."

"They've got Mumford and Sons. It's not the same."

He finished his pint.

"I could do with the company."

Jake's eyes glazed. Niamh shivered. It wasn't Jake alone. The students on her course – they too had been ignoring her. They'd been staying in class when the teacher finished, delaying without packing up their bags. They'd waited until she was gone. Packed a second time, rather than being outside on the pavement, her presence contaminating them.

Niamh said, "Tell me, how's your blog coming along?"

"They shortlisted it for the Costa Book Award."

"But you're still writing?"

"They're cunts," said Jake. "He's not interested in you, she isn't coming back for me."

"They shouldn't be together."

He said, "And whose fault is it that they are?"

A moment of hope, the Millbank protests, had been and gone. The coalition government had survived. Niamh had stood watching one of the marches through central London, the women with studs in their noses, the boys with their red banners fluttering behind them. Cops preparing in the side streets. Remembering all that hope now made her feel old. She wanted the same things she always had – but wasn't sure they'd happen.

At the first seminar of the year, Niamh didn't dare hope the Salt Professor would whisper, "How could anyone be so tall and so good at History?" Her heart had been beating like a dragonfly trapped inside a glass. She knew there was no realistic prospect of the Professor wading over. "That question the woman asked. Yes, her with the thin arms, and the hair like Ophelia. There's a job going in the department, and it's hers if she wants it."

The Salt Professor earned his name after a question he'd asked, "What was the most valuable commodity in a fourteenth-century kitchen?" He'd said, "Come on, people." He'd asked, "Didn't any of you read the chapter? I copied it for you." When no one had replied, he'd scrunched his nose and said, in a strained voice, "Salt, the answer's salt."

One of the boys in her class had been worth thinking about. Him, the one doodling, Liam. Six foot one, handsome, with calves like a footballer. In a room full of guys too old for their acne, one at least was presentable. She could see the future: they were going to share a tub of caramel ice cream. After that, he'd smother her in kisses.

One evening in October, Liam had taken her for a date. They'd met in a pub, the same Chapel Bar she was sitting in now. Niamh remembered the look on Liam's face as she walked in. He closed the copy of *Private Eye* he'd been reading, a glint in his eyes as he rose, pulled up a chair for her. Their one night together, how he'd talked, his granny with her flat above the post office, the fights he'd survived at school, how Stockport had been falling to bits even then, and it was worse now. She'd said to him, *Let's see a film.* The movie was going to be some superhero flick, utter nonsense, but she didn't care. A film would be proof of commitment. *Sure*, Liam had said. *Why not?* He'd left his pint unfinished on the table.

In the pub, a woman called last orders. Jake left. It was a period of numbness which became a chasm of time as the bar emptied around her. Someone turned the lights off and on and off again. Niamh left too. She'd assumed Liam and Aitch were long gone, so it was a surprise when she caught them, two blocks down, slinking towards Caledonian Road. They seemed so happy, lost in themselves. She hung back in the shadows, waited till she was sure they hadn't seen her. She followed them down Penton Street, then walked behind them as they meandered down the hill, turned left, right, and left again. The city was seething its midnight blackness.

They were doing that thing new lovers do, smooching beneath an old London plane tree because they'd never kissed there before, spooning like teenagers because they'd never kissed on that paving stone. Inching forwards, they reached the canal.

Niamh followed them, crept as close as she dared.

She heard Aitch say, "I'm going in."

He said, "You mustn't."

There was something else she didn't quite hear – he had his back turned to her. Niamh crouched down, her hands still, keeping as quiet as possible.

"It's March. March counts as spring, doesn't it?" said Aitch. Her voice was clear. She turned round and looked back at Liam as she spoke.

He didn't seem to answer. Or if he did, it was with a look. That little smirk he had for when things went wrong. God, how he'd pained her when he smirked.

Aitch bent as if to roll down her jeans, slipped and fell. Her hands clattered on the paving stones. "Ow," she said, performing hurt – a toddler remembering to cry after falling.

Niamh's breathing was so loud.

Liam said something about sewers. Or that's what it sounded like.

"How dare you insinuate I'm drunk," Aitch said, "when I'm as sober as a jug." Niamh grimaced. *That bloody woman.* Aitch hadn't misspoken, she'd meant it as a joke.

He said. "The water's filthy."

"It'll be the two of us." Aitch discarded her top, pulled off her jeans. She dived into the water. Then, out of it she broke – whooping with delight at her own bravery, "Wow!"

"Your knee," Liam said. Then something that could have been, "You're bleeding."

"Come in. Show me how much you love me."

At Aitch's command, Liam lifted his sweater from his shoulders.

The thing was–

It wasn't easy to admit even to herself but, for days, everything had been wrong. At one point, there had been no more than two people who knew about Niamh's *shame*. Two of them were capable of being the source of the story. Aitch and Liam – no one else had known. One of them must have started the rumour, it couldn't have been anyone else.

That was the speech that Niamh had been preparing to deliver. She hadn't yet confronted him, but she would. *She would.* She was going to tell him he was a prick-stick, that he pretended to be better than the other guys, but he wasn't. That he'd ruined her life. That he'd made her life a misery and she couldn't ever forgive him.

Aitch burst out from the water, hooting with laughter. "You're missing out." Her face made such a perfect image of happiness; it was enough to make milk curdle.

Never, ever, would Niamh forgive her – or him.

Liam said something compliant. Then, with fast, awkward-looking movements, he removed the last of his clothes.

Aitch was still grinning, "Did you see the way she was gawping at you in there?" At that word, *she*, Niamh froze. Aitch continued, "Can't we hook her up with somebody?"

Don't you dare take pity on me.

"With Jake you mean?" Liam's voice was unenthusiastic as he continued, "It isn't always easy being Niamh."

All evening, she'd sat there like a lemon, wanting to know which of them was the source, and not daring to ask, but now she could hear them laughing at her, she felt the rage rising. As soon as they were on dry land, she'd have them.

Aitch's face ascended out of the water. "Come on," she urged Liam.

"I'm glueing it," he said. Doing it, she decided. His words were fuzzy, as if she was the one who'd been swimming, and the sounds came to her through liquid.

He was down to his boxers now. Niamh couldn't help but sigh a little. She'd dreamed of seeing him naked, and here he was, almost close enough to touch.

"You'll love it in here," said Aitch. To prove her point, she lifted her arms and let her weight carry her beneath the surface. Till all you could see by the light of the streetlamp was ripples on the water's surface. Aitch leapt from the waves. "It's as warm as a bath."

Liam splashed his heel into the wetness, cried out, "It's *freezing*." Niamh took another look at him in the water, that torso. "I don't believe you've got me doing this." He looked good even when he was shivering, waving his arms to keep warm.

There was a smell in the air. The canal stank of iron, of something else, too – a deep, rich, odour like rotting seaweed. The muscles at the back of Niamh's neck tightened.

"You goose. I'll swim to the other side – then we'll go."

"Ok" said Liam, "sure." She didn't quite catch the words, but she could hear the tone with which he said them – his voice wrenched out of shape.

Aitch dropped her head into the water, began a short crawl, lifting her head on the second stroke, the third. Her feet were slow, then fast, chopping through the murky liquid.

Niamh could hear a sound whispered in the darkness. It was her name. Someone was whispering it over, and over.

Don't be ridiculous, she thought, it's the *wind.*

Out of the corner of her eye she caught someone, a woman. The stranger was old, thirties or forties. She wore an old-fashioned dress, black as ravens' feathers. A shawl on top, the outfit softened by a lace collar. The woman looked strong. She looked severe.

Please God, Niamh thought, *don't let the crazy woman speak to me.* Her heart was pounding like a bass drum.

The woman looked at Niamh, smiled a crooked smile. "Good morrow, cousin."

"Hi." The word made a little squeak in Niamh's throat.

She looked down towards her feet. She was telling a silent prayer to the Gods, *Make this end, make this end–*

When she looked up, the woman had moved on. Niamh was standing behind a cluster of three trees – her shield against suspicious eyes. She put her hands to her cheeks and breathed out in relief. *Thank goodness*, the black dress had vanished.

She took a step to her right. Beneath Niamh's foot, a twig

cracked. In the sleeping city, the noise was a loud as a gunshot.

"Who's that?" Aitch shouted. "If some pervert's getting their kicks out of this–"

"It's a thing," said Liam.

Aitch growled, her head bobbing in the water. Then off she went once more, swimming across the canal. When she reached the far bank, she rested for a moment, placed a hand on the concrete barrier. "Isn't this great?" she shouted.

"Sure," said Liam. Something about going back.

For a moment, they were silent. All Niamh could hear was the sound of water dripping, the wind stealing at her hiding-place. That smell of decay.

Then, in the distance, a movement. From the other side of the canal, a sound so soft it might have been a kiss.

Niamh saw, or thought she saw, the woman from before. Without discarding her black dress, she dived. In the darkness, her movements were smooth. The water parted without protest at her touch.

"Hey," Liam said. "Hey," he said again, his voice cracking. His head lurched back, forwards. It struck the water. Niamh rose, crouched back down again. She didn't dare reveal herself. Liam splashed out a helpless fist, cried out in pain. He flailed in the water. Liam kicked back against his invisible adversary. He screamed.

A hand slithered out from the water, grabbed the hair at the back of his head. It dragged him struggling, down into the darkness.

Aitch stopped, paused for an instant, then dived into the water, raging, fighting the liquid, lifting her eyes towards where Liam had been. He escaped for a moment, was pulled again below the surface. Niamh's heart raged, readied to burst.

Aitch shouted out his name, beat on the water with her fist. No answer.

Once again, Niamh was begging the Gods, begging fate, beginning anybody who'd listen to her. *Make him all right. He's got friends. He's in class on Monday. Don't let anything bad happen to him – please.*

A spot on her cheek. Soothing rain.

At last, Liam's body rose. Ten metres downstream from where he'd been. His jeans buttocks surfaced first, then his shoulders. The backs of his heels bobbed in the water.

Aitch reached him, grabbed him, fought Liam's body, turned him face up. She pinched his nose, tried to CPR him. She struck her shaking hands against his unmoving lungs. "Help me," Aitch screamed, saying the words not to him, but to the world itself as it watched, and listened without answering. "You, whoever you are. I know you're there."

Niamh couldn't answer. The rain came faster. It fell like petals, made her clothes damp. She wouldn't stay there. She couldn't. Behind the trees, she stood. She started to leave. Against all her better instincts, Niamh turned for a moment and looked back.

Behind her, Aitch's fingers were reaching for Liam, she'd managed to turn him round. Niamh saw a red, raw, patch of skin missing from his face.

She could feel an egg in her throat. It was trying to explode itself upwards, outwards. With a heave of her shoulders, she let the evening's celebrations go.

"Help me," Aitch begged. "*Please*."

Niamh forced herself upwards. Out along the road, she ran.

CHAPTER 2
SHAME

Niamh climbed onto the bus, paid with her Oyster, squeezed past the men ogling at the front. She found a seat on the top deck. She sat there in the cold, in the darkness, playing PJ Harvey, Patti Smith, Bikini Kill to herself. Her iPod was running low. Niamh switched it off. She hadn't seen Liam drown. She hadn't. She'd imagined the whole evening. The night had been one long hallucination and if she could get back to Vron's, throw herself into her bed and hide there, all would be well by the morning. She'd had her reasons for being angry with Liam, but those had been normal feelings. They had nothing to do with what she'd seen. *What she hadn't seen.* She pinched the skin below her thumb, ground a nail into its fleshy softness.

At Vron's, Niamh scrabbled with her keys at the door. Dropped them, picked them up, stabbed them at the lock, screamed when they wouldn't go in, clamped her mouth shut. She opened the door; heard it slam loud enough to raise the neighbours two doors down. If she could walk up that flight of stairs, so long as she didn't wake Vron, she'd be safe. *Shit.*

It wasn't the evening that was making her so clumsy – or not the evening alone. It was Vron, too. Even in good times, the woman made her feel helpless. It was the volume at which she talked. It was her Dolce & Gabbana sunglasses, her Bandolier bag, her white Dior sailor's pants. It was the gold rings she'd squeezed onto seven of her fingers.

Vron had never told Niamh her age, not that Niamh was

about to ask, but her landlady was old enough so that she no doubt dreamed in black and white. Her children were on their second or third rounds of university. Niamh was making up for their absence. Darling, she called Niamh; she was always trying to persuade her to join some late-night party. The absence of her children caused Vron to play the part of surrogate mother with Niamh as her honorary infant. There would be a new restaurant, a talk at her club in Mayfair, and Niamh would be her plus one. She invited Niamh in deference to her youth, as if her tenant would have the energy to stay out late, and yet they both knew that Niamh's preferred routine was staying in and reading. Niamh always endured the party for an hour before at last making her escape, but not tonight. Tonight, Niamh was going to force herself sober and take charge.

Niamh kicked off her shoes. She went up the stairs, on which Vron had left out the clutter of her day – little ceramic plates, half-drunk glasses of wine. Niamh glared at the debris, tried to summon the energy to glide through the assault course.

Niamh placed her foot down, hoping she'd avoid the traps for the unwary, in case she stood on something painful, cried out, summoned Vron from her room. You're late, darling, Vron would say, not disappointed. She could have lived with disappointment. No, Vron would be eager. She would demand all the gruesome details. As if Niamh was the sort of person who went out at night, danced the evening with strangers, returned rejuvenated at dawn.

Niamh was halfway up the stairs now. There was nothing beneath her feet. Nothing, until her foot nudged a saucer. Nothing worse than a plain porcelain dish. It didn't break, but it made a little ringing sound. She shrank back, she squeezed her body against the wall to escape the sound. Please, she begged, stay in your bedroom. It's nothing.

She waited in the darkness for the silence to form, snow obscuring a footprint. Niamh had made it to the top of the stairs. Two strides and she'd be in her room. Two long, confident, strides. She would close the door behind her. If Vron woke, it wouldn't matter. So long as the door remained locked with Niamh on the far side, she'd be free.

There was a single obstacle between Niamh and sleep. The barrier was a cat. Black, bristling. She could see his eyes studying her. Her landlady had two of them: Rahab, and Tirzah. For a moment, Niamh wasn't quite sure which of them it was.

"Hey, stranger," she whispered, in a futile imitation of comradeship.

It was Rahab. She recognised his green eyes, the brute strength of his shoulders.

"Shhh," she whispered.

She knew what to expect, "Cclll," with an intake of breath, Rahab would hiss his authority over the corridor. But that wasn't what happened. He showed her a welcome he'd never granted her before, lay on his back, offered his stomach at her,

Desperate for her bed, Niamh bent down. She pressed her face so close to the cat's that, with one swipe, he might have scratched her nose. "Scat," she ordered.

Rahab ran away, abandoning his kingdom.

"Niamh Malone," Vron called out. "There's no need to bother that poor beast."

"I wasn't," said Niamh, her heart sinking to her hips.

After that, Niamh and Vron were downstairs in the kitchen. The little treasures on the side, the green jade disk. She placed in front of Niamh a tumbler with three fingers of Piña Colada and an ice cube. "That'll warm you up," her landlady said.

"Thank you."

Vron said, "Have you seen a ghost?"

"Why are you asking?"

"The look on your face. I thought some sweetheart had come back to haunt you."

Niamh touched the drink to her lips. It was so sweet, a milkshake for grown-ups. "I'm tired, that's all." She forced herself to smile.

Vron liked to think she was generous. She needed to hear the gratification of children, friends, lodgers, telling her she was kind. In receiving her gifts without showing proper enthusiasm, Niamh was putting herself in a box marked, "thankless." That was the thing about their relationship and the presents Vron gave her. The more Vron gave, the more she expected. At Christmas, Vron had taken her to see Swan Lake at Sadler's Wells, the Muscle Mary dancers with their oiled pecs. The tickets had been £30 each, and Vron had paid. Which was kind of her until you remembered that every week Niamh was paying £500 in rent. For which she received a room so small that the bed overwhelmed the floor. From that perspective, £30 once a year was not the act of extraordinary generosity that her landlady reckoned it to be. Niamh had felt her heart skip a beat when Vron had said, the week following, "The papers say young women are being taught how to write thank-you letters."

"Aren't we over all those old rituals?"

"Beyond good manners? Darling, *never*." Niamh had taken the hint, bought proper lined paper, scrawled her gratitude in her neatest handwriting. Her landlady nodded her assent.

Now Vron was doing the dishes. Her face was thick with white cream, not yet absorbed into her skin. On her hands were marigold gloves – plastic, daytime things shouting the contrast between their new cheapness and the expense of Vron's Yves Saint Laurent nightgown. She said, "Your friends, I can't believe they'd abandon you when it's freezing out."

Translation: Liam and Jake were useless. There was in the world no more than a single person who was sympathetic to Niamh, her kind-hearted landlady.

She said, "No one abandoned me. They didn't–"

Vron had filled the sink with water from a kettle, with so many suds that the bubbles floated into the air. Putting down her tea-towel, she said, "In my day, we used to expect that a young man would walk you home after you went out promenading."

"It wasn't a date."

"Darling, you don't need to hide anything from me."

"It wasn't."

"Well, whatever you got up to, I see precious few signs that your gentleman-friend went to any trouble to make sure you'd eaten."

Vron waited for Niamh to answer.

Vron said, "He does put himself forward, but I like him."

As her landlady spoke, Niamh released a little, unintended, sound. Less than a sob, more like the noise a tap might make if you loosened it. The sights and sounds of the evening were coming back to her, the scream Aitch had made. Would have made, hadn't made.

"I hope nothing's wrong," Vron said, her lips curled in disappointment.

"I'm fine."

"My poor darling," said Vron, her look chiselled from granite.

Vron demanded the truth. In any normal circumstances, Niamh would have been happy to oblige. She hated it when she had to fib. Not for any moral reason. More because she wasn't any good at deceiving. Whenever she lied, she blushed. It was her blonde hair, her light complexion. She reddened like a beef tomato.

At last, she had an idea. Not a direct lie nor the complete truth, but something that would run sideways and between them. Niamh said, "You know that feeling when you're in bed, and you have a nightmare, and you wake up, and it feels like the dream was real?" She held a hand to her face, felt a blissful chill there.

"What sort of a dream?" said Vron, her look scrutinising Niamh's clothes for clues, her shirt with the tear at the sleeve. The mud on her socks.

"I was sleeping," said Niamh, holding her back straight, ignoring the first tingling in her cheeks, "and Liam was there. We were in a park. We were by the canal, and he made me get in with him. He was swimming. Then something went wrong." But nothing had gone wrong. "I watched as he fought the water. The thing is–"

"Yes," said Vron.

"When I woke, I was convinced he'd drowned."

Outside, the rain had grown in strength. It lashed down, battering the windows.

Niamh said, "I knew it was a dream – but it all seemed so believable."

She could taste the damp in the air. She could smell its thin, squalid, presence, the intrusion of ditches and sewers into the evening.

She said, "You'll tell me I'm a dunderhead, but it wasn't until I'd woken up that I realised it was nothing. Nothing at all."

"Use the landline," Niamh's landlady replied. "Call him. It's late, but if you explained."

"I don't want to be the sort of person who calls when

they've had a bad dream."

"Oh, darling," Vron said, putting down the bottle of Fairy Liquid, and taking a step towards Niamh, who gave a sad little smile, inched backwards on her chair. Vron must have sensed Niamh's reluctance because she turned, picked up a tea towel. She resumed her chores.

Niamh finished a second drink. The pineapple was too sweet, as if it had stewed for a decade in its can. She opened a third.

When Niamh looked up, she realised that Vron was talking. Her landlady was showing her a further kindness. She was avoiding the topic of Niamh's dream. "I thought you'd have to go back to your mother's," Vron was saying, "in the summer, but it seems like Antoine won't be coming home after all. He's got other plans, you see."

Vron waited for Niamh to answer. She pressed on, "Isn't that good news? You and I, all June and July. No distractions."

"What awful fun," Niamh said, her heart sinking.

Antoine was Vron's eldest child, the true owner of the room of which Niamh was the mere temporary occupant. Vron was proud of her son, she always said so. You could hear it in the way she pronounced his name, *Antoine*, as if she and her eldest child had been sitting a moment ago in a field in Provence eating peaches.

"Antoine's going somewhere nice?"

"Sorry?"

"In the summer, I mean?"

Vron said, "Enunciate girl. There's no need to shout," and she gave Niamh a very tolerant look. "I'm not some old biddy you need to scream at."

Niamh wrenched her mouth into a semblance of a smile.

"You've got children to look forward to," her landlady said. "Happens to us all. They finish their exams then they flee. All the love you give them – it counts for nothing in the end. When your child goes away, it's a death. Afterwards, they never ring you."

"But you enjoy the quiet, don't you? I remember you saying–"

Vron removed a handkerchief from her sleeve, blew her nose in it. "I had been hoping there might be someone to look after me when I'm old."

"You're not old," Niamh insisted. "You won't be – not for years."

Vron glared at her. Then she seemed to relax. She poured another drink. Vron said, "And there's a new man asking after me, very distinguished bloodline."

Niamh had a feeling as if a pair of spotlights were following her. She tried to say something anodyne. She heard a can opening, saw its contents as they poured into her glass. The thought of her bed no longer seemed quite as welcoming as it had.

"I'm being selfish," Vron said. "Burdening you with my life, when it's your friend you were worrying about."

She was pressing for more. It was the unspoken price of their conversation, Vron would contribute as many cans of alcohol as Niamh needed. In return, she needed to provide a sob-story, the material which Vron might share at the next party she went to.

"I'm not concerned. His girlfriend's with him."

"Girlfriend? I thought–"

"We weren't ever an item," said Niamh.

Vron grunted, her eyes trapped between disbelief, and disappointment.

"*We weren't*," said Niamh.

The room, already cool, turned that bit colder.

Here were some of the places that Niamh would rather

have been. In London in 1381, before the peasants descended from the countryside. In the same city in 1665, awaiting the arrival of the Plague knowing that half the people around her would die. Or there again in 1666, experiencing the Great Fire, the destruction of her home, and of the homes of all the other people who'd survived the pestilence. In 1940, before the Blitz. Any of those times would have been preferable to spending the evening trapped in Vron's kitchen.

Niamh felt a pressure on her to speak and yet, grey and fuzzy as her mind was, an instinct guided her to caution, the memory of other times when she'd let Vron see her weakness, and afterwards the landlady had used it against her. Like the time Niamh mentioned her sibling, Yvonne. She'd been talking about her mum, and how her mum couldn't stop going on about Yvonne. The next morning, Vron had asked her, *How's your sister? The favourite*. The words had been a slap to Niamh's face – her face had reddened, her eyes stung. Or there had been another moment when her landlady had asked what she'd do with her degree and Niamh had said she'd write books. She'd said that she was good at writing. She hadn't forgotten the little flare of the old woman's nostrils. Her look of disbelief.

Niamh said, "He's on my course. Isn't that enough?"

"Is it?"

Niamh was feeling sick. She put down her drink.

Her landlady wanted her to reveal more of her suffering, but Niamh wouldn't gratify her. Even letting the memories take shape in her head was too much. She'd not intended more than to ask Liam the question: who was it who'd been gossiping about her? Was it him, or was it Aitch? Because you didn't need to be Sherlock Holmes to know that one of them had started the rumour going. If it was Liam, then he needed to learn his lesson, that's what she'd been thinking.

Until earlier – the canal. It hadn't been her fault. *It hadn't.*

Niamh said, "He's one of the better ones."

"The life, and soul of the party, darling," Vron said. It was a phrase she'd often used before, always of herself. Hearing the same words now, with the dark outside, the rain nearby, they seemed to Niamh cold, dismissive.

"I wouldn't say we ever dated, but we did go out," explained Niamh. "We went to the pub, then a film. He came round here first – that's when you met him."

"I wished you a very pleasant evening."

"You did. You were so kind to us."

"Nonsense," said Vron.

Niamh wasn't going to tell Vron about the aftermath of her date with Liam, how she'd thought of him as the one who was going to sweep her off her feet. He was smart, he was funny. Most important of all, the way he'd looked at her. She knew he fancied her something rotten. She'd lived for months on the memory of his greedy expression.

Vron said, "I'm an old woman, and there are some things I've learned. I've seen the best and the worst of people. I'm telling you, there are more men out there than you'd think."

Niamh was remembering the evenings when Liam hadn't rung. She'd sat at her table, staring at the landline. She said, "I'm sure there are."

"That's the thing about men. You reckon the last one you had was the best one. Your final chance of love. But they're like fishes. Thousands of them, all swimming in the sea."

Niamh swallowed. *Stop*, she wanted to beg. *I know you're trying to help, but it's not doing any good.* She said, "It's late. I ought to–"

"When my Quentin died," said Vron, "I learned it's never too soon to start dating. I started looking in the personal columns after four days. I wasn't ready, but I did."

"Four days?" asked Niamh swallowing. Liam wasn't dead. *He wasn't.*

"Darling, if you're asking me how I coped – I felt liberated."

"But you loved him. You did love him, didn't you?"

Vron's eyes opened in disbelief, that Niamh could ask the question. "With all my heart," she said.

CHAPTER 3
THE TWO WIDOWS

A day passed and Aitch was sitting at Vron's kitchen table, covering her cheeks with trembling hands. Niamh was doing her best to help, even as the words formed and broke in Aitch's mouth. She told Niamh about the paramedic who'd come to the canal. How he'd taken out his flashlight, pointed it at Liam's face. Dropped the light, said *Mary, Mother of God*. Put what he could of the corpse on a stretcher. Hidden Liam's body beneath a blanket.

Niamh had gone to sleep telling herself again that she'd imagined everything, that Liam was fine – she'd see him at university on Monday morning. Before Aitch had spoken a word, Niamh could see it had all been lies. Seeing her friend with the tears streaming down her cheeks, her eyes dull, her mouth gaped open. That had been enough to make Niamh admit she'd deceived herself; she'd known the truth all along. He was gone. Liam was dead, and, if there was any rightness in the world, she should be grieving her hands to her face as Aitch was doing. For she'd lost him, as her friend had too. She, like Aitch, should be distraught and yet her eyes were dry. Some instinct held her sitting there, rigid.

The police had tormented Aitch with their questions. How long had she known Liam? Had they fought? How did she explain his wounds?

"Wounds?" said Niamh, fearing that if she said nothing, she would give the impression that she had known about them already – when she hadn't. *She hadn't.*

Aitch opened her hands in confusion. "I don't know, it's what they told me. They showed me a photo," she said. "An animal raked him with its claws." Her jaw wobbled. Aitch said, "I don't know what I told the police. I know what they asked me, but not what I said."

Aitch's eyes drooped, she shook herself awake.

"You're exhausted."

"A bit, I guess."

"Why don't you go and lie down? My room's spare," Niamh said. "When you feel better, you can tell me everything."

"I shouldn't. I don't want to impose," said Aitch. She stared at the cup of tea which Niamh had poured her. She'd left it so long, it must have congealed. She said, "I'm struggling to remember everything I saw. It's as if a part of me doesn't want to know what happened. It's as if my brain has been trying to protect me."

Niamh said, "I've got a temazepam."

In the end, Aitch agreed. She curled up on Niamh's bed. She lay on her side, with her eyes open. Niamh switched the light off, closed the door behind her.

It was a book that had brought Niamh to London, Malone's *History of England.* It was an antique, with scuffing to the covers, corner-bumping, copious stains. "He was your great-grandpa times three," her dad had said, after she found the book in the shop in Erdington. When life was against her, Niamh went back to Malone. Published in the Port of Glasgow, Cameron, and Ferguson, 1837. Today, Niamh needed it. Malone was on the landing, where she'd left him. He was her shield against all the strangeness of the world. *Into the blessed Island, there came sailing from Troy, a Queen, Albine. She had no equal in strength or stature.*

She sat there at the stop of the stairs, thumbing with desperation from page to page, hoping to find something, anything, that would take her away from what had happened.

"Niamh?" said Aitch, from inside the room. She called out her name a second time, loud enough so that she rushed to the door.

"What is it?"

"I can't see him. I close my eyes and try to remember what he looked like. I can't see him. I'm telling you, I can't see him–"

"It's all right," said Niamh, bending down to hold her. "Go to sleep. You're exhausted. You'll see him in your dreams." She was ready to tell her guest everything, to throw herself on Aitch's mercy, but her friend's breathing calmed. The room stilled.

Niamh went downstairs, set to tidying away last night's cans. She picked up the glasses, washed them in the sink. Niamh couldn't stop remembering Liam. He had been all knees and elbows in class. He argued with the others when there was no point. Didn't seem to care how much he riled them. He accumulated enemies without caring. One time, another of the boys said something about not judging the past by the standards of the present, you wouldn't expect Victorian England to have all the answers to climate change.

You don't think, Liam had said. *You don't think industrial Manchester was a party? The air thick with pollution, half the kids dead before they were fifteen. They didn't care about the environment?* She remembered the other boy's face, twisted in hatred.

Liam had broken all the rules. He wasn't supposed to speak back. The others had been to private schools, or to one of those London academies where every parent was a doctor or a lawyer. They had the deeper knowledge – of the weight of a silver fork in your hand, what it feels like to wake up in a four-poster bed, the taste of red wine that an ancestor put down in their cellar a hundred years before. Against the knowledge the other students had inherited, all Liam had was books. The others teased him with an impression of shallow friendliness, "Liam, mate." He was meant to accept his place in the ladder of creation, several rungs below them. A member of the servant class, he was intended to be seen but never heard.

Niamh had always seen Aitch as self-obsessed, needy, like a thirteen-year-old girl with a bag of aniseed balls in her pocket, but she'd been in the house all morning and she hadn't spoken a word of self-pity. Niamh knew that people rose in adversity, and all Aitch had in front of her was suffering. The other students would hide from her, wouldn't know what to say. They'd stare at the ground rather than speak to her. "I'll be the exception," Niamh told the empty kitchen. "Even if you become a grumpy bitch, I'll always be your friend."

When Aitch woke, she looked around the room like a hunted animal. She rejected all offers of food and drink. "I thought I'd feel better but I'm worse. I'm sick. I ought to get back."

"You shouldn't be alone," said Niamh. "Not after last night."

Aitch paused for a moment, seemed to waver before deciding. She reached to her wrist. She said, "It's his watch." She loosened it, held it out as a gift. "I've got a Garmin of my own. If I keep the watch I'll lose it, but you can have it - if you'd like."

"I couldn't."

She held her hand out. The watch inside it. "You were his friend, too."

"I'm so sorry," said Niamh, hating herself as she took it.

The watch's face had cracked. That afternoon, she went to have it fixed. The woman in the shop made her fill out a form. It wasn't an Omega or any of the fancy brands they displayed in glass cabinets. The woman couldn't promise they'd be able to mend it. They'd have to send the watch off, and the watch was going to cost fifty quid, no, that was the price of the deposit, it was going to be seventy-five pounds on top of that to sort the glass. She'd need to pay a round two hundred to repair the lot of it. "Do it all," Niamh said, "I don't care how much it costs," but when she checked her balance, she couldn't afford to mend the watch, not till her loan came. Niamh explained that the money was due any day. The woman smiled, acted like it was normal behaviour to see a customer staring at her bankcard, swearing at herself.

Niamh went to the bathroom in Vron's maisonette, turned on the water. She sat beneath the liquid, her knees and her chin sticking out. The dampness scraped her skin. After ten minutes it was cold, so she let the water drain out. Then she filled the bath once more. A third time, she filled it. A fourth. Outside, the day gave way to night.

She struggled against her grief, waded in its headwaters, felt herself swept away, caught up in currents stronger than she was.

These were some of the places she'd gone to with Liam. One Saturday in the autumn, they'd taken the bus to Highgate cemetery. They snuck through the railings, dodging the entrance charge, found the plain grey tower beneath which George Eliot rested. They'd gone for food at the Turkish-German-doner kebab place, where they put too much onion in the salad. It hadn't been a date. They'd paid for their own food, not had a single drink. But, already, she'd been thinking. Hoping. She'd had a fit of giggles she couldn't explain. She'd been imagining what it would taste like, her breath stinking of onion and his too.

Then there was the time, a week after that, when they'd met up in Hyde Park with the mission of teaching Jake to ride a bike. It wasn't a mystery, he said. Everyone else had learned and he hadn't wanted to. He'd never felt the least desire, and now he did. They'd taken turns to hold the handlebars, grappling with him, clinging to stop him from falling over.

Jake and Aitch had gone for a coffee and next thing Niamh and Liam were both on the bike, her hanging from the top of Liam's shoulders as he raced till his face went red and he couldn't stand. "Backy!" Liam shouted, when they caught up with the others. "Backy!" he cried, like a schoolkid on the first day of summer.

"I can see," Aitch had said, her eyes wrapped in barbed wire.

Behind him, Niamh had cackled.

The University's Vice-Dean for Student Welfare said the reason he'd called the meeting was because they needed to decide about Liam's room. By a decision, he meant *free up the vacant unit*. Let someone new live there. Make the choice that Liam's mum had refused, had passed on to them. Niamh was squeezing her hands into fists, forcing herself to smile, knowing she shouldn't say anything that might upset Aitch.

Niamh spoke, "What we're saying is that it was his room. He paid for the whole year's accommodation. It's still his, even if he's dead."

"Look," the man replied, "We got a waiting list with five hundred students on it. How am I helping Liam if I leave the room unoccupied?"

"It sounds like you've made your decision already."

"I'm saying – you need to get on with your lives."

"It isn't unoccupied," said Aitch, "I've slept there every night since he died."

"Did you hear her?" Niamh said. "No way. We don't give permission."

They walked back in silence to Aitch's room. Niamh sat there for a while, waiting for criticism. She knew how it would go. Her friend would say, *I hope I don't come over as ungrateful, because I'm not*, and those words would hang in the air, dark as crows' feathers. She'd say, *but,* and that "but" would stab Niamh in the heart.

Aitch said, "I've tried talking to him, you know. I've tried everything, but he doesn't come to me, not even when I'm asleep."

Niamh said, "I'm sorry."

"Why are you sorry? It's not your fault."

They sat together for a while, two friends against the world. Then, without warning, the temperature dropped. Aitch was studying Niamh and scowling. She was preparing to speak, thinking the better of it, summoning the strength–

Something was coming. Niamh said, "What's wrong?"

"You shouldn't be here."

"What?"

"He wouldn't want you here."

"What's going on Aitch? You're scaring me."

"He never liked you."

"We were friends."

"That was his watch, wasn't it?" Aitch said.

Niamh looked down at her wrist. She smiled. What a funny mistake her friend had made. She said, "Don't you remember? You gave it to me. I'm having it fixed." She looked up, waiting for the lines to smooth in Aitch's face.

"I never said you could keep it forever."

"You did, the day after he died. You came round to my place, and–" Niamh stopped. The way Aitch's nostrils had flared – it scared her.

"I don't give a shit what I said. I'm telling you now, I want it back."

"What?"

"Back. Now."

"All right," said Niamh, "What's up with you?"

"Don't come here again."

"Don't be like this, Aitch, please."

"Me? You're talking like I'm the problem. Me? When you're a thief. He would never have trusted you – you *bed-wetter.*"

"Don't do this," Niamh begged.

But Aitch wasn't listening. "I knew there was someone watching and I didn't know who. It was a puzzle – until Jake worked it all out. You were at the canal, weren't you? You'd stayed behind, hadn't you? You were the one watching when Liam drowned–"

Niamh wanted to say, *it's true*. Nothing would have made her happier than to throw herself on her friend's mercy, and say, *I did. You're right.* Instead, she made herself strong. She said, "I don't get what you're banging on about."

"You could have helped him. I tried to help him breathe. You could have come out from your hiding place, we could have dragged him out of the water together. You could have rung the police with me. But you didn't do any of that, you wouldn't lift a finger. Instead, you stood there spying on him. Then you ran off. Well, I hope you enjoyed what you saw."

The crack of Aitch's hand broke the silence. The blow to her cheek kept Niamh warm, and heat was so much better than the cold, the silence, which followed. Better than the tears in class, in the supermarket. At home. Better than the looks from her classmates.

No, Niamh explained to the woman from the shop, when she rang. *I'm not having it fixed. I shouldn't have bothered you.*

Niamh had never been a regular swimmer. At secondary school they'd made them all take a lifesaving test. The rules were simple: they had to manage two lengths in their clothes. If at any point their feet touched the bottom, then they would have to suffer a year of remedial swimming lessons. Niamh had suffered the examination, fought the weight of the cotton top and shorts, had collapsed at the end of the test, dry-heaving at the poolside.

Swimming was her mother's sport. For many years, Niamh had endured it, had gone along because it did no harm. More than once, she'd sat beside the water, reading, glancing up from time to time to peer at the adult bodies, the men who needed fifty strokes to complete a single length, the women with their cellulite and their grim determination.

Now, though, she felt a need to be near water. She found the wetsuit her mum had brought for her, packed in hope. There was a reservoir an hour from Vron's maisonette. Niamh set her alarm to wake at six. She paused for a moment in the painted brick changing room. She felt the shock of the cold dampness as it slipped down the back of her wetsuit, she lifted her face with a stifled scream into the sky. There was something splendid about the silence beneath the water. She was trying to make herself as thin as an eel. In the vast expanse of the cobalt greatness, she swam breaststroke, her head bobbing beneath the surface – two slow, patient, strokes before she breathed again. She chose breast-stroke because that's how it was, the best way to swim outside, her mum had taught her long ago. Keep your head up because you don't have the security of the lanes painted on the floor beneath you.

She remembered the steel finality of Aitch's hand upon

her cheek. She wanted to apologise, but to whom should she direct her regrets? The way Aitch saw it, Niamh had offended against both her and Liam. The living she might assuage, she might put a card under Aitch's door, buy her some Dairy Milk. She could apologise for everything, promise never to wrong her again. But it wouldn't be enough, now Aitch had given herself an excuse. Aitch wasn't fighting for her own grief, raw as it was. She was fighting for Liam.

Then it was the day of the funeral, and Liam's mother said she'd drive Niamh. No one, it seemed, had told the mother about Aitch and Niamh's one-sided war. She wouldn't have gone but Liam's mother wrote to Niamh, phoned her, said she'd found her name in Liam's address book. She said that at Christmas he'd told her about all his friends, told her they meant the world to him. They were in the car now, and Liam's mother – fifty-something, woollen green hat, spectacles so strong that her eyes loomed behind their glass barrier – was saying, "I don't like to complain about good weather, but I'm finding this challenging."

She had an envelope, money for Aitch, who made a brief show of resisting. Liam's mother said, "I want you to go out this evening, go to his favourite pub. Have a drink on him." She said, "The way I see it, so long as his friends remember him, he's still living."

Niamh was on the back seat, not daring to raise her eyes from the floor.

Liam's mother said, "I'm so grateful you've made it."

Aitch said, "And we're glad to be here."

"Me too," said Niamh, hating herself, how weak she sounded.

Jake was sitting beside Niamh. He must have noticed her squirming because he turned and stared at her. She blushed, looked away. "Thief," he whispered.

Liam's mother must have heard something because she turned her eyes to the rear-view mirror. "You're the one who's building planes, aren't you?"

"Designing them," he said. "Dropping them, crashing them. Balloons, helicopters, paragliders. If it falls out of the sky, you can blame me."

Niamh couldn't recall the last time he'd been so talkative.

Jake made himself all *Thank you, Mrs Thorne. Of course I will, Mrs Thorne.*

Liam's mum said, "I'd rather you called me Deirdre."

Next thing, they were in the crematorium, in a little room by the chapel's side. When Liam's mum said she'd go and powder her nose, Jake brought out a flask of cherry brandy and offered it to Aitch. Niamh watched as Aitch buried her head in Jake's shoulder.

Jake was telling Aitch, "You won't be alone. Not now, not ever."

"I'll leave you to it," Niamh said, closing the door behind her.

She prayed when told to. Niamh listened to the sermon, watched the clip of Liam at Christmas, when he'd been a kid. She waited till all the other mourners had left. She rose. She walked to the coffin and left on its top a gift for Liam. Niamh laid a white carnation on his coffin, whispered to the wooden box. "Miss you, dickface," she told him.

And she did. She mourned his clothes, his grin. She missed the days when he'd been so kind and gentle to her – like a piece of glass so fragile that if you left it out of your sight, it would crack. She remembered how she felt in the build up to their big date, how convinced she'd been that he was the one. She even missed that last evening. As full of rage as she'd been, and bitter recrimination. The song of the machine, "FIGHT." The conviction she'd had that if she talked to Liam, there'd be some innocent explanation. Even now, she still believed in him.

"Miss you more than anything."

A hand reached past her, lifted the carnation from its resting place. "Don't you dare," Aitch said. "Don't you fucking dare."

Niamh was looking at her friend, her former friend, as the day swam around her. The chapel, the wooden walls behind them. In a weak voice, she said, "I didn't– Wait– Why?"

"You shouldn't have come. He's not yours, you didn't own him. You didn't do anything to keep him alive. You don't get to decide what goes in there with him."

Aitch was standing over her, staring, with the power of a woman wronged. She took the carnation, walked with it to the desk and the round metal bin, over which she dropped the flower. It dropped, hit the lid of the receptacle, fell out and onto the ground.

Aitch let out a scream. She kicked the bin so hard she dented it. She kicked it again. "Now get out."

Running, panting, Niamh did as she was told.

On the grass outside, a middle-aged woman asked if Liam ever wore sunglasses. Niamh wasn't sure. It had been autumn when she'd met him. The woman said, "I'm Patrick's mum. You'll have heard Liam talk about him. They were inseparable."

Niamh nodded. Her heart was squirming inside her chest.

The woman said, "Patrick has this story about how Liam bought this pair of sunglasses. Liam was sixteen, and all that summer he went everywhere in mirror shades. So that if anyone smiled at him, that's what they'd see, the world smiling back at them." She said, "Liam was such a sweet young boy, one in a million."

"He was," said Niamh in a weak voice.

She walked to the stone bench, sat studying the clouds. "There you are, darling," Vron said, her face brightening at Niamh's approach. "What a delightful eulogy."

"His poor mum," said Niamh, who still felt sorry for herself.

Vron sat down on the bench. She paused. She said, "My dear, you must tell if I'm speaking out of turn, but that friend of his, the one with her waist showing–" Vron meant Aitch. "I've been meaning to say, of all the decades of the past to plunder, the thirties – that's an odd one to choose. On a day this cold, never."

Niamh felt conscious of a generational duty to defend Aitch. Without any enthusiasm whatsoever, she said, "Everyone dresses like that."

"That's the other problem," said Vron. "All rather common, isn't it?"

Niamh started to protest, but Vron spoke over her. "And the little looks she was giving you, the way she talked about you when you weren't listening."

"Her name's Aitch," said Niamh, "and she's fine when you get to know her." If it wasn't the literal truth, she needed it to be true.

"I've seen women like that before," Vron said. "Committed to their own narrow way of seeing the world. No good deed goes unpunished, that's what my father used to say. And that boy of hers – he's every bit as bad as she is."

Niamh looked up. Aitch was moving through the crowd, shaking people by the hand, smiling at them. Jake was with her too, but keeping a respectful distance, as if his most important duty was to preserve the dignity of the innocent widow.

Through the crowd, the two of them went, accepting greetings, smiling at strangers, accepting with good grace the sympathetic words offered to them.

Niamh said. "You never understood my friends. You always gossiped about Liam." As she spoke the words, she watched Jake touch Aitch's arm. He looked up and saw Niamh watching. He leered at her.

Her heart, which had been in the vicinity of her hips, fell to her knees. Vron said, "If I asked about him, it was for your sake. Darling, you can call me a foolish old woman if you like, but the two of you seemed happy together."

Niamh said, "Aitch is my friend, don't make me fight her."

CHAPTER 4
THOSE HIDEOUS BOYS

A week passed. In a dream, Niamh was a kid again, clumsy. "Always falling down," said a woman's voice. Niamh looked up and saw a great black cat. She followed the panther through the empty house. She and the creature left by the back door. In the garden, there was a pond. Willows hung over it. The panther told her to dive in. The night was quiet as she reached the pool's edge; in she went, abandoning herself to the water. She swam beneath the surface, face down, breathing through the gloom. Her eyes were open, studying the depths. From out of the liquid darkness, strange creatures came to meet her. The first was a leech and it pulsed as it swam, looping and stretching and changing its shape, like an animated pair of tights. The others were combs and rainbows, sea wasps, sea walnuts, living water – shapeless bodies, mouths, limbs like string. They twisted their sinews as they moved, their warm tentacles.

Liam hadn't been Niamh's first date. There were all the boys who'd liked her at school, given her a piece of their chocolate, the joke from a Christmas cracker, who'd kissed her, their tongues tasting of Dr Pepper. She'd had lovers too, Oliver Wooton, Amelia Gower, Ava Hillard, Joseph Oliver, Charlize Cooper. None of them had been lasting passions, more than one had been embarrassing as hell. Niamh had learned that she liked men, women, *whatever*, people who looked after themselves. Take Charlize for example, Niamh had gravitated to Charlize because of the way she carried herself. Short, in no sense willowy, but secure in herself, her eyes flashing fire should any of the boys come too close. Charlize had been Niamh's shield-maiden. When things with Charlize had been at their best, what Niamh had wanted more than anything was to be her. They'd gone into sixth form in each other's clothes, Niamh in Charlize's sailor boy top, Charlize in Niamh's sea-green blouse.

She could remember Charlize, curling down over her, her back arched, her teeth open. She could remember the moist warmth of Charlize lips, the touch of them against the tender skin of Niamh's neck. On their second date, Charlize had told Niamh she had anxiety. She didn't make it sound important; for a year it wasn't and then it was. Niamh had found it devastating to watch as Charlize's fire burned out. As the incidence of Charlize's non-attendance from college increased. As her parents flailed from non-solution to non-solution. Cognitive Behavioural Therapy, changing A-levels midway through. Deferring the exams.

Their relationship reduced itself to sitting on pub benches, waiting for the second drink, the numbing third.

Sixth Form the next morning. A boy with pimples (Grant).

The boy, "So, you two, yeah? Do you?"

Niamh, "Do we what?"

Grant, "You know."

Niamh (aggravated), "No, I don't know."

Grant, "Well, do you?"

"Piss off."

Those boys – summoning their memory from the abandoned vaults of the past was a way of avoiding the most unwanted thoughts: that Aitch hated her, that Niamh couldn't even claim the moral satisfaction of victimhood. Niamh deserved it. *She deserved it.* Aitch was right, Niamh had sat there watching. She'd done nothing to stop Liam's death.

She went back to the scene, saw how narrow the canal was, how small and shabby. "I'm sorry," she said to the water, to the boats, to the still of the morning. "I could have saved you. I should have." And the other thing Niamh had forgotten: not the trees overhanging the canal, not the flower beds, they didn't count, the other thing she'd forgotten was the bridge at the water's end, the tunnel beneath the road, its dark opening. She stood by the bridge, waited there, a useless thing. She dropped down to the bench.

She was thinking about the date they'd been on, the autumn before, how nervous Liam had been. When she heard herself saying "Let's go see a film," the words had sounded desperate even to her, needy. He hadn't looked at her but kept his eyes on his pint, his best-loved companion, blessed Niamh with a desultory, "Sure."

But this was her memory playing tricks on her, she recognised. The first part of the evening had been fine, the trouble had come afterwards. The film – Niamh had come out of it overflowing with joy – and she'd made to kiss Liam.

He'd jumped.

For God's sake, she wasn't making this part up. Liam had *shot into the air* at the prospect of her lips touching his. "I'm sorry," he'd said. "I – I wasn't expecting. Let's try again if you want. I don't mind–"

There were darker depths to that evening with Liam. God, her memory was unforgiving, that's what mourning did to you, it brought the dead back to life. It was like swimming in the dark. You hold your breath, stretch out with your shoulders until you're among creatures so far below the light that submarines couldn't find them.

She'd tried to leave, and Liam stopped her.

"Can we have another drink?" he'd said, and she'd had visions of redemption.

They'd necked a beer, her head reeling with the chance of them becoming an item. They'd slaughtered another Guinness, Liam's words echoing with possibility.

She'd asked, "Can we do this again?" her legs squeezed tight together.

"I'd be happy to," he said.

They'd drunk a third and she'd felt a pain in her side – a stitch, a knot of tension – she'd wanted to stand and relieve herself ("Where's the pisser anyway?"), but she didn't dare end the moment or separate herself from him.

"If you want," he'd said, "sure, tomorrow." And she'd wanted his interest, she'd wanted him to commit. Any moment, he'd ask her back to his.

"Niamh," he'd told her, and it wasn't the words, it was his tone. They were sitting together, between them they'd rescued the evening, when she put her hand on her leg, and it was wet, and she was eighteen years old for Christ's sake, and what were her kidneys doing? She'd gone and wet herself, hadn't she? She was still pissing herself even as she looked at her jeans, smelled the tell-tale smell of sugar.

She'd never forget how he'd looked at her. The shake of his shoulders, the little, uncontrolled, sideways movement of his jaw. Like he was the one – not her – who felt her shame. "Jesus," he said, looking at the state of her trousers. The words echoing round the pub.

That was why he hadn't rung. Because she'd embarrassed him. He didn't want to see her. That's why'd he never called – because she'd changed her phone, because she'd given Aitch and Jake the new number, but not Liam.

Things didn't get any better after that.

In the days before he'd died, the rumour had travelled round the uni about their date. Some hint had escaped. It was the Thursday of the week before Liam died and Niamh had gone to class, as usual. One of the boys came into class late. He could have sat in the chair beside her, instead of which he'd walked the full length of the classroom to keep his distance. The boys had smirked in mutual understanding.

She hadn't known what they were getting at until, in the break, she drank a Fanta from the machine. She went to the toilet. Graffiti covered the back of the cubicle. *Niamh the Leaker*, the first of the authors had written, in a red pen, *Malone the Drip*, in black, with a series of dots cascading down the door. The baby Aristotles had competed to invent the most humiliating nickname for her, *Piddler, Pissypants, Tinklebelle*–

Sitting on the bench, the midday sun cold above her, Niamh swayed. She had to fling out a hand to stop herself from falling. The boys that had suffered at the hands of Liam, they couldn't touch him, so they had their revenge on her instead.

Why had she come here? She couldn't explain–

She remembered how Jake had treated her that last evening in the pub – his coldness. He must have known, Aitch too. The whole university knew.

There were two people who could have started the story. Liam was the likeliest. That's why she'd been looking for him that evening. The Thursday of the week when Liam died. She'd needed to confront him. If he was the one who started the rumour, then he could stop it. She'd been on the verge of confronting him when–

"Shitstain," she said–

A thought had trespassed into her consciousness. What if it hadn't been Liam? Four months had passed since their bad date, four months in which he had known her secret and kept it hidden. No little giggles in lectures, no shouting her nicknames out of windows. Seven days before he died, he and Aitch had started dating, and that Thursday she'd seen herself on the back of the door, the crude drawing of her grin in her moment of unwanted release. Aitch must have asked Liam what had happened on the date, he'd told her his new love some version of the story. She found out and within a day the whole university knew.

The air was damp now, the clouds dark, and heavy with the prospect of rain. Niamh sat on the bench beside the water. "I'm sorry," she said out loud, and she didn't know anymore who she was addressing, Liam or the younger version of herself, the worst evening of her life.

She listened to the whisper of the water as the wind passed over. A woman sat down on the same bench as her – leaving a small gap between them. The woman wore a black dress, its thick material looked heavy, damp somehow. Her hair was thick, blue, and black, as coarse as old rope. Her dress stank of dust, decay, of puss oozing from a wound.

A bag-lady, Niamh thought, and yet – the woman was powerful, imposing, the thick muscles of her shoulders visible in the bunching of her dress.

"Do I know you?" asked Niamh.

And, even as she asked the question she remembered. Niamh did know her. Of course, the night with Liam – the woman in the black dress.

Niamh felt herself redden. "Go away."

The creature had turned to face Niamh, was watching her. There was something masculine about the strength of her jaw. While her pupils were so black they obscured the iris, like the sun in an eclipse. Niamh could see the pain of the city reflected in those eyes.

Niamh said, "Leave me alone."

The woman was still staring at her, her eyes harsh and unblinking.

"I don't know why you're here." The creature in the black dress was staring, a predator still as it tracking its prey. Niamh looked down at the ground. She said, "Haven't you done enough to ruin my life already?"

The woman didn't flinch. When she spoke at last, her voice was soft, "I came when thou didst call to me."

Niamh said, "I didn't. I never–"

All the sights and sounds were coming back to Niamh – Liam, the water. "Get out of here," she said, the hairs on her neck standing to attention. In response, the woman looked about as troubled as a child unwrapping an ice cream.

Niamh rose to her feet, made herself as tall as she could. She pointed her finger at the strange woman's chest. "Leave me alone or – I don't know what I'll do."

The woman stood. As she did, Niamh realised the futility of the situation. The woman was broader than her, taller. Six feet, at least. What was Niamh expected to do? She couldn't have fought her. Niamh's legs were shaking, her feet leading her away, "You need to know, I don't believe in the living dead. Or monsters. Or things that go bump in the dark. You're figments of the imagination. I'm not scared of you."

"Dost thou trow me a ghost?"

"Go," said Niamh, squeaking with fear, and desperation.

The woman took a step back, gave a little sad smile. "I do not mean thee any harm. How could I? Thou wast the one who summon'd me to this place."

"Leave," Niamh ordered.

"We shall speak again."

"Not if it's up to me."

After the woman had left, Niamh waited by the waterside. She shivered. She waited long minutes until her breathing had slowed.

She looked up and down the canal. She knew there'd be

other victims. A creature like that must produce more victims. If she waited long enough, the survivors would come and sit on the bench beside her. Their grief would be as hungry as wild dogs, their shame too.

CHAPTER 5
FROM STATUS TO CONTRACT

That evening, Niamh lay on her bed. She stared at the ceiling. She swore to herself, "Shitting, shitting, shit." She needed someone to confide in, but who? Niamh grabbed a notebook off her table, found the first clean page. She wrote, "Liam." She crossed him out. On the second line, "Aitch." She scratched that one out too. On line three, "Mum?" The inclusion of the question mark was the giveaway. Niamh put a line through that choice. "Yvonne," Niamh preferred the sound of that one. To show her confidence in that choice, she drew an emoji :-) to the side of her sister's name. She smiled for a moment at her own lopsided drawing, but then she gave a little, sad grunt. No way could she talk to Yvonne. Her sister was avoiding her. She was in Aberdeen, neither answering her calls nor responding to texts.

On the fifth line of the page, Niamh wrote, "The Samaritans." She knew that was a duff idea before she had finished writing it, they had worthier cases than her to trouble them. On line seven, she wrote, "Vron." Line eight, "Salt Professor." Line nine, she left blank. She closed the book and opened it. She squeezed her eyes shut and opened them. She turned the book upside down. Still line nine remained what it had been, a void.

She crossed out the Professor.

That left a single name on her list – Vron. "No," she said. "No way am I asking her."

But when she looked at the names once more, Niamh

found it hard to avoid the inevitable conclusion. Against all her better judgment, she had made the least bad choice – her scheming, often generous but always self-obsessed landlady.

Having made the decision to speak to Vron, the next task was how to prepare the conversation. Niamh could have opened with a plain statement of what was bugging her. *I'm sorry Vron, I've brought a weird, violent, water spirit into my life, and I could do with some advice about how to send her to Hell, if they'll take her.*

Niamh respected Vron's survival instincts; she doubted that her landlady had the relevant skills to help her. Fight the magical creature? Talk to her? Report her to the (non-existent) magical police? Vron's answer would be, *See if the woman's free next Friday. There's this new boutique opened, and they do embroidery for Louis Vuitton. I'm in their diary with a plus one and I would appreciate the company.*

"You'd go shopping with her? You're mad," Niamh realised she was speaking out loud. *Stop it.* She grimaced. If there was one thing worse than carrying on a conversation about a fantasy woman with her landlady, it was imagining the questions that would follow. Already she could see Vron shaking her head, not in anger with Niamh but disappointment.

The last of the evening's light was illuminating the dust on her bedroom wall.

Niamh stood, fiddled with her bedroom switch. She left her room, knocked on her landlady's door. Not a sound. She remembered Vron's hints about her new man, but she was too old to be shagging some stranger. Niamh's feminist consciousness perked up in response to that. Hey, *Sister, since when did you start dumping on other women's dreams?* But she hadn't, she wouldn't – *I didn't mean it, don't curse me.*

Before, when Niamh dreamed, all nature had welcomed her.

This evening was different. She found herself once again in the strange unfamiliar house where she'd spend the previous evening. Again, she left the mansion, again she found herself in the garden with the pond. The moon was high above, the sky lit with stars. She waited in the water to see if anyone would join her. The dampness closed over her and down she dropped, into the depths, the slime, the rotting ooze. The leaves surrounded her, the creatures closed above her, cut off the last shimmer of the light coming from above, left her struggling to breathe. Into the depths they pulled–

When Vron came downstairs for her morning coffee, which was not before eleven thirty (how come the older generation got away with late nights?), Niamh was in the kitchen waiting for her. She made a plate of scrambled eggs, with wild Atlantic smoked salmon, sourdough loaf. Vron ate every morsel without complaining.

At last, she turned to Niamh, "Is this about the rent?"

"I'm on a standing order, you know that."

"You're feeling guilty? It's not a good look, staying up all night, waiting for me to come in. You're my tenant, that's all. There's no need to pry. I don't need to justify myself if I'm out, having fun, with a gentleman friend–"

Niamh felt a headache. "I didn't stay up all night."

"Your light was on."

"I fell asleep reading."

"Still," said Vron.

"Don't be like this," Niamh pleaded. "This is serious. It matters to me."

Niamh's challenge was to persuade Vron to listen for a minute without adding questions of her own, interruptions or asides. She began by asking Vron if she'd noticed how sad Niamh had looked, how caught up in herself she'd been – for weeks. Vron said, "I go to the gym for that." She'd discovered the leisure centre at the end of the road, and there were fitness instructors there and for £50 an hour (a snip, darling), she'd found this woman who'd worked on her core. Vron needed Niamh to know that there was no good reason to worry about her. She'd been improving her pelvic floor so that she wouldn't have problems with leakages down there in her years to come. Vron said that it had always been one of her most profound beliefs that good physical health did more than make you fitter, it was good for the mind too. The answer to Niamh's moods, she concluded, was more exercise.

"I swim," the young woman said.

"Once a fortnight, darling," said Vron with a sniff.

"That's not fair. The last week, I've been going every day."

Niamh tried again. She asked if Vron remembered about the dream she'd told her about in which Liam had died. Vron did. She thought it was the saddest thing she'd ever heard. She said it made her think of that novelist, what was his name, who'd predicted every detail of the sinking of the Titanic, even that the ship crash into an iceberg. "He didn't," said Niamh, who'd read the same article in the papers, left it for Vron on the landing. "He thought it would crash into another ship." Vron said, "Oh, darling, you're serious, aren't you?" She said, "All that history you've studied, you should be making documentaries."

Niamh said, "The premonition–"

"Why don't you pour me a drink?"

Cursing herself, her meekness and pliability, Niamh obliged.

The alcohol seemed to relax Vron a little. She told Niamh that she was earnest, wasn't she? That Vron didn't understand the youth of today, how solemn they were in every situation. Vron told Niamh not to pout at her like that. She said, "You need to talk to someone else. I'm a gadfly, darling. I'm frivolous. Women in my generation never learned serious. Ask my children, their demands always make me so uncomfortable."

Niamh had a class at 3pm but decided to skip it. The Post-Colonial Matinee Idol would be teaching the course. He wore a red scarf and a blue bodywarmer, and he looked to Niamh like a man who'd cashed in an accountancy career. He'd have taught himself French from a cassette, and by some outrageous turn of the wheel of fortune he'd swung the job of teaching them History. Niamh tried to recall what she was thinking when she'd chosen the degree because whenever she thought about him, his anecdotes, his dropping of the names of famous writers he'd waved at in the street, her doubts were too many to mention.

She sighed. He wasn't the problem. It was Jake, it was Aitch. She couldn't risk going back to uni and have them laugh at her. Nor, for that matter, the boys in her History class. She recoiled at the memory of the drawing, the toilet door.

She needed something to get the tension out of her shoulders. But she couldn't go anywhere outdoors, not after yesterday. What if the woman in the black dress was still following her? The water spirit wouldn't get on with chemicals, Niamh reckoned. She was a creature of fresh streams, not of chlorinated lanes.

Niamh made her way to her leisure centre, checking as she entered the building the creature wasn't stalking her in the reception area. She changed, chose the fast lane on the right, slipped into the water. Around her, she could feel a hum of people – a children's group in the learner pool, adults in the lanes to her left, a man already half a lap ahead of her. As she eased into a front crawl, it seemed to her that she was swimming faster and with greater ease than before. All those laps outdoors must have done her some good. Her shoulders engaged the liquid, with each stroke she stretched a little further. Stroke, stroke, breathe–

She turned back. For the first time in days, Niamh felt her body relax. She was swimming well and she didn't feel tired. She was wondering how many lengths she'd finish that day. On other days, when she'd gone into the pool, she always swam at least twenty laps, but twenty laps wasn't enough for her today. The pool was twenty-five metres long, which meant sixty-six laps in a mile. Today she was going to swim forty-four laps of front crawl.

She turned again. Niamh could feel the strength in her hands, in her feet. She straightened her legs, felt them loosen at the ankle. With each kick, her toes pointed. Her feet felt so large, as if someone had attached flippers to them. Her legs were moving in that perfect rhythm where each kick was making her go ever faster.

Ouch. She felt her arm strike something – was conscious of the shock a second or two before she'd made sense of it. Not something, *someone*.

She was in the deep end. The man in front was shouting, "You, what the hell were you doing? Are you blind?"

She clung to the lane marker. "I'm sorry."

The man had a jaunty, blue swimming cap and oversized swimming goggles, with a brand name printed on their top. He was taller than her. Muscles burst from his upper arms. He said, "This isn't an Olympic pool and if you want to join a swimming club, you're going to need to learn to take more care of the people around you."

She apologised a second time.

Bit by bit, she was piecing together what had happened – she'd swum into his foot. That's why her arm hurt. She felt her hand beneath the water. At least she hadn't sprained it. She understood why he was shouting at her. He wasn't a bad swimmer, he fancied himself. By swimming into him, she'd offended that most fundamental rule of pool etiquette. The bit they never need to put in the printed rules because everyone knows it already. Not, *Don't leave your lane* (she hadn't, she'd swum in a straight line). No, it was the rule which said: *Every woman must always swim at least ten per cent slower than every man.*

She didn't know what else to say. She'd apologised already, hadn't she? How many more times was he going to make her say sorry?

"Lifeguard," the man shouted, waving in the direction of the boy who sat there.

"Please," Niamh said. "I know what I did was wrong. I know how distressing it is when you're swimming in your lane and you're trying to relax, and some idiot comes blundering into you. I didn't mean it; I'm sorry. It won't happen again, I promise."

It wasn't her call to make, she knew that, but she reckoned it was a good apology. Waited for the man in the blue cap to accept it.

She wasn't going to say this out loud, but a part of her was feeling quite proud of how fast she'd been going. She looked at those shoulders on him, wondered how often he'd stalked some poor woman, followed her length after length, until she stopped, left the pool and gave up the lane for him. She wouldn't have liked to say this out loud, but if Niamh had outswum him – wasn't that a victory, of sorts, over the patriarchy?

She played her last remaining card, "Please don't make a scene, I haven't had a great day." There, she'd given him a chance to be a gallant. *Take it.*

She was thinking of the boys in her History class, of Aitch, and Jake. She was even thinking of Vron. It felt like they were standing in the pool behind him.

"Lifeguard," the man shouted a second time.

Smiling, the boy said, "What's wrong?"

"*This woman* needs someone to talk some manners into her," the blue cap said. This woman, he spat those first two words, as if what he'd meant to say was *This crazy bitch–*

The lifeguard peered down. "Niamh Malone, fancy that!" Then, his face creased in thought, "You weren't widdling in my pool, were you?"

She walked through the back roads of London, past the tower blocks, through streets of low-rise housing. Her heart felt huge in her chest. It had been three weeks since she'd seen the woman with the black dress and it felt like three hundred; there had to be a way through, but she couldn't find it. She fought to extract herself from the passages that led nowhere, until she came to a railway bridge, to abandoned shops, their white-painted fronts a canvas of competing messages, tags painted in red, in pondweed green.

She remembered the first time Liam had come to Vron's and sat there talking. It hadn't been a date, not yet, but he'd listened. She'd told him about her ancestor Malone, the author, the tradition of past generations, and that's what she thought about History, it was like gardening, either you had *green fingers*, or you didn't.

Niamh chose the walkway, the trees watching over the water, their roots tearing through the concrete. She found the tunnel, wide enough for boats to pass, its teeth twelve grey stones built into a mouth of brick, and at the far end of the mouth, darkness. She sat on a bench, the sky bright above her, but cool, damp, the perfect May morning, and there she waited, remembering Liam, mourning the two of them together.

From the bag on her shoulders, Niamh brought out a silver hairbrush. It had been a gift from her mum. She felt the city retreat into the distance.

Niamh shivered. She sat by the tunnel, the water beside her feet. She looked again at the hairbrush. Engraved on its top were three initials. J. D. M. The J and the M carved in a fine hand. The D worn away. M for Malone.

From beneath the weeds appeared a face. The woman stepped onto the land. Forwards she came, walking as silent as a fox. The woman twisted her neck one way then the other, then shook the water out of her clothes.

Niamh studied the woman, the familiar black dress which covered her body from her arms to her ankles. Her face was pale, with a violent red tinge to her cheeks which conveyed not health, but decay. She saw the past in the thick forest of lines at the base the creature's neck. In the unremitting blackness of the woman's eyes.

She kept her mouth in a steady grimace. Her teeth were uneven, some long, some short, all sharp. Between them flourished knots of moss and weed. They made Niamh think of a crocodile, its mouth open for its prey.

The woman said, "I did not reckon on such a speedy return."

"You told me I'd come though, didn't you?" She waited for a moment before continuing. She said, "I'm lucky, I guess. The others, they're feeling it worse, the recriminations after he died. It's changed them, and not for the better. I've lost people who meant a great deal to me, but why aren't I hurting even more? I loved him."

"If thou say'st so."

Niamh said, "His death wasn't supposed to happen."

The creature asked, in her deep voice, "Suppos'd?"

"Fate, I mean. Karma. Some things deserve to happen, and others don't."

"And thou consider'st thyself the skeptic?"

Niamh blushed. The conversation wasn't going to plan, "I didn't want him to die."

"And yet thou didst call me," the stranger said.

"I didn't," Niamh said. "No."

The woman turned from her. "I cannot undo his passing."

Niamh worked on the brush, polishing it against her jeans. She said, "I wanted to speak to him, there was something I needed to ask him. I never asked for the violence."

"Thy rage was sweet as blood. It raised me from my bower."

Niamh swayed on her feet. Making herself strong, she said, "I brought you this." She took the creature's long hair in her hands and worked the brush down it. Niamh teased the worst of the knots apart with her fingers, then eased the brush down them.

She watched the lines on the woman's neck as they opened, as they closed. They weren't a sign of age, she realised. They went the wrong way, at an angle, parallel to her collar bones. Out they opened, and in they closed, each time the creature breathed.

Niamh said, "What made you like that?"

The woman said, "Do my looks discontent thee?"

"Not at all." Niamh gave the brush to the woman. She touched the monster's wrist, as smooth and cold as fish-scales. She watched as the creature took the brush and worked it through her hair. Niamh saw again the woman's shoulders – how strong they were.

Niamh wasn't scared. Her body was calm, her heart slow. The first time she had seen the creature she had felt an irresistible urge to run. Not this time.

She said, "My name's Niamh."

"Bold Niamh," the woman answered. "I am Jenny."

Niamh said, "Please, will you help me?"

CHAPTER 6
CREEPS

Over the days that followed, Niamh learned a great deal about revenge. Jenny, it turned out, was a skilled practitioner of that art. For there were in London at this time any number of abusers, braggarts, bullies, cocks, conformists, crawlers, daddy's boys, dullards, egotists, misogynists, narcissists, offenders, perpetrators and pimps, not forgetting the women who were expected to endure them. Jenny watched the young men, the ones who went to the gym, who sucked in their stomachs and blew their chests out. She waited for the women to speak. She helped them when she could. The women were white, black, Turkish and Greek, young, old. Their faces were full, were gaunt. Some of them rejected Jenny's help, floundered in her presence. Several refused her help. One died, came back to life afterwards, and wandered the streets of the city, a red sash dangling from her neck. Others accepted Jenny's help. They asked her to play the role of bodyguard, judge, or vigilante.

The victims offered Niamh a grudging tolerance. She made a point of never offering words of advice – the men did that, giving their opinion in haste, telling the women to diet, to change their clothes, drink more, drink less. Jenny came to the women when they were alone. They walked through the city, and Jenny went among them, talked to them, listened, promised little and did much.

Tiwa was twenty-three years old. She had been born in Wood Green, left, and returned. She had a job with a publishing company. Her manager was a thief. Their business's north American owner had paid her manager a seven-figure sum to rent a second set offices in Lancaster Gate. He had found an unwanted, abandoned building. The rent was a fraction of what he'd declared. He chose to pocket the difference. "You tell anyone about this," he'd said, in a voice as calm as the sea on a summer day, "anyone – and I'll kill you."

Once a month it was her job to go into the building that her manager rented. The office was filthy. Pigeons had broken in through the windows and roosted in the abandoned desks. Birdshit lay on the floor like a disordered blanket, clustered upwards in glinting stalagmites.

The first Friday of each month, Tiwa returned home after unlocking the doors of that office, after walking up the glistening stairs, with the birds soaring away from her, upwards to the higher floors, into the roof and out through the holes they'd made.

Through the next week, Tiwa would lie on her bed, her chest so tight she couldn't breathe. The pain drilled in her head, her body was cold – shaking. She might be there a few days. She might be there two weeks. When she returned to work, the next inspection was already booked in her diary. She tried writing to her manager, tried phoning him. He was in Cannes. He was at Ascot. The next time, when she rang, he answered. He told her to calm down. "Let's face it," he said. "You aren't going to make a fuss, are you?"

Tiwa walked along the side of the canal, whispered Jenny's name.

Into the derelict office Tiwa walked. Her face was held tight. She had with her a box of matches, a scrunched-up ball of newspaper. The fire burned the copier room, it incinerated the plaster ceiling. It danced on the floor, turned the offices into ash.

The rains fell, washed away all remnants of the blaze.

Niamh let her feet dangle in the water, held them there long hours at a time. The ragged-dressed woman sat beside her, soothed her feet in the canal. It pleased Jenny to have Niamh there, to share with her a companionable silence. Sometimes, the creature would sink into the darkness, rest for a while beneath the still water. A great flurry of air-bubbles would rise to the surface and Niamh was left wondering if Jenny was speaking to her, sharing a language of clicks and snorts, unconcerned that Niamh did not answer.

Niamh put a hand in the water, held it to her cheek, let the drips fall to her shirt. Around her, the city was going on its way – all the busy people.

When Niamh took her feet out of the water, her soles had become a mass of grey, puckered whorls. Beneath the joints of her big toes, opals had formed. They had dots in the middle, like eyes. She kept her eyes on Jenny, on the woman's wide shoulders, her broad arms. Niamh touched her own upper arms. She could have sworn that they too were changing, growing firm. The dampness was changing her. She was so supple there, so clumsy on dry ground. Even her eyes were changing under the water's influence. Darkness was less of a hardship to her than it had been, sharp daylight a heavier burden.

Niamh slept in, had to endure Vron's cajoling. Vron told her she needed to tidy her room; said it was her turn to cook. But the complaints seemed to come to her from a distance. She wanted to eat from her fingers, needed salt with her food.

Jenny gave Niamh the name of a primary school in Hackney. The school had served the same community for more than a hundred years. Niamh hired a car, sat inside its new-smelling interior, watched as the day meandered to a close. At quarter past three, the building was alive. The children were in their classrooms, their bags already packed on the desks beside them. On the near side of the school gate, a crowd of parents waited.

Niamh removed from her bag the silver flask Jenny had given her. The contents were nothing unusual, ordinary London water. She had a little porcelain dish – onto its surface, she poured the water. She watched as the liquid pooled on the dish. Then Niamh spoke the words of summoning: “Jenny. You will come in my need.”

There was no rush of sound, no blinding light. The greatest change was nothing more than a certain feeling, a tension in the air, the build-up of pressure before the rain falls.

Niamh closed her eyes, “Who am I even looking for?”

Mirelle Jones is the maid's name, said a voice in her head.

“Where is she?” Niamh asked. “How will I recognise her?”

Until this point, Jenny's instructions had been sparse, nothing more than the school's name. She hadn't even told Niamh when to be there.

“Give me something to work with.”

She closed her eyes again, felt the day passing all around her.

“Come on,” Niamh slammed the steering wheel with her fist.

Outside, the sun reflected off the leaves.

Niamh hunched down behind the wheel. She waited. Ahead of her, the gate opened and a uniformed child so small she must have been in year one was running towards a woman who was a grown-up replica of her, cornrows matching. Others followed: the infants proud of themselves, too big for kisses, the older ones tolerating their elders.

Niamh was looking from mother to sister to teacher to child. There would be a survivor in this crowd, one whose pain had summoned Jenny's interest. Niamh saw one of the pupils, blonde, her schoolbag stuffed with books, and the man who had come to collect her. She saw the girl's sullen refusal to make eye-contact with him. A movement distracted her. She studied the line of middle-aged teachers giving words of encouragement to the last of the stragglers.

She looked to the right, saw a tall, copper-skinned teacher. She was wearing a bulky blue dress, and over it a brown and white necklace, and above it she had the most glorious smile you could imagine, a look of satisfaction in her day's work. She was hugging the last of the departing children, sending them back to their mothers with a wave.

"Mirelle?" she whispered. The word began in her mouth as a question, but as soon as she said it, Niamh was sure it was her.

The day darkened into evening. The teachers returned to their classes, marked the children's answers. Mirelle and a colleague went from class to class, tidying up the rooms. At last, the colleague left. Through the rooms, Mirelle worked, switching off lights, locking doors.

Niamh would have sworn that Mirelle was the last adult in the building, but as she approached the school-gate, keys in her hand, a man appeared to her side. He was older than her. He wore a tweed blazer, carried a leather briefcase.

"I'm tired," the man said. "Will you keep me company?" The street was empty, the words clear.

Mirelle made some excuse.

"One drink couldn't kill you," the man said.

Niamh counted to a hundred, followed them to the pub. She didn't have much experience of following people, didn't want to stick out. There, she ordered a Guinness because it would take the longest to pour. Niamh waited before raising her eyes, looked around the premises and taking her drink to a large armchair in which she could hide.

Bentley was his name. He told Mirelle stories about his working day, how he'd stood up for all the teachers, the head had had some terrible plan, and he was resisting her. He talked about the man he'd been when he was young; he'd played in a tin-pan band, they performed at the Carnival. He'd been a hellraiser, got drunk, at work too. He'd taken drugs. Bentley was talking about this dealer he used to have – when he was in his 20s – all the weed he used to smoke. There was one variety, and he shook his head. He pinched his thumb and forefinger and laughed at the memory of the grass and at the crazy, wild, young man he'd been.

He bought Mirelle a vodka and orange. A double, he told the man behind the counter. For himself, he ordered a coke. They reached the point in the evening where the questions demanded an answer – where next? Would there be a next?

Mirelle seemed to like Bentley. She still had the same attentive smile she'd had all the way back at school. She laughed at his jokes, the ones that didn't make her groan. That said, he was quite a lot older than her, twenty years older at least. This act Bentley was playing, this memory of the wild young boy he had been – Niamh heard the stories, weighed them against his ironed shirt and expensive suit – knew Mirelle must be making that calculation too.

Mirelle said she'd enjoyed the evening. She told Bentley she needed to go home. It was her turn on the cooking roster, she'd promised her flatmate.

"Sometimes, that woman could take a back seat."

"I promised her."

Good on you, sister.

He shrugged, was magnanimous in his defeat.

Niamh waited till Mirelle left, watched Bentley finish his coke. He was very particular in how finished it. He took the lemon out of the glass, placed it on the table. He picked out the ice cubes and scrunched on them.

"Well, this has been a wasted evening," Niamh said.

As she spoke the words, Bentley turned in her direction for a moment. She flinched down into the armchair, hoping he hadn't seen her.

Bentley stood, left by the same exit as Mirelle.

Follow them.

When Niamh left the building, a slow, steady rain was falling.

In the distance, Bentley was striding along the pavement, a determined look on his face. He was getting away from her. She hurried to keep up.

Mirelle was fifty metres further on, walking so fast she was running. This was a quiet area – warehouses, car repair shops. Some closed for the evening, others boarded up.

Does she need me?

"How would I know?" Niamh answered. Then, at once, she regretted her words. It seemed to her the evening was a test and she was failing it.

Mirelle turned, saw Bentley. As she looked back, Niamh could see her face. The smile had gone. Her face was gripped in fear.

"Get the bastard," Niamh said.

Bentley moved toward his victim. Even as he did, a creature in a black dress was there, grabbing him by the arm, jerking his body to the side. He crashed into a skip. He fell, screamed in pain. The sound was stifled all at once, as Jenny placed her hand upon his mouth.

"Tush now," Jenny told him.

CHAPTER 7
THE GEOGRAPHER

One afternoon, Niamh was studying the building to which Jenny had sent her. *You will discover me Edward Sanden*, Jenny had said. Niamh set to work, investigating the task. Soon, though, it became clear that this was something different from Jenny's usual requests. Labouring through the various search engines revealed no more than a single person with that name and they'd buried him somewhere up north, four hundred years ago.

"Why him?" Niamh asked.

"Edward Sanden of Sanden Hall," Jenny answered, her eyes two ebony stones.

Mirelle Jones was spending her days at Jenny's canal-side, arrived there before Niamh, remained there longer into the evening. She joined in the conversation.

Edward Sanden's name was spoken, repeated. It seemed to Niamh that she was being assessed, and, like the last time, she was falling short. As if the river creature ascribed to her powers of investigating and finding skills that not even the internet could supply.

"He's been dead for centuries," Niamh complained, staring at Jenny as she did. "There's nothing to find."

From behind her, Mirelle Jones's voice came. "Look harder," she said.

Tom Sanden was Niamh's first lead. His front door was blue, fragile-looking, unremarkable save for its brass knocker with a lion's face. The beast stared at and beyond her, angry, frightened, in its declining years.

Tom was in his seventies. He'd worked in local government, environmental prosecutions. He'd been a student once, Warwick. Focusing on his course, not the protests. Geography, you could see it in the images she'd found – his waterproof, his Specsavers glasses. She reckoned he dreamed of returning to his studies, exploring the Peak District, taking photographs of the moraine, the drumlins. Making annotations on an Ordnance Survey map he'd kept since the sixties. Like her dad if he wore Moss Bros, had autumn in his soul.

She'd met with Jenny at the canal. The creature had trailed her hand in the water. "This encounter – it is within thy power?"

"I'll be fine," said Niamh, bristling inside. It was bad enough when Vron doubted her, even worse when Jenny did.

Niamh had asked Jenny where she slept, what she ate, how she had become what she was now. The water spirit said no more than suited her. She acknowledged that she was not from London, was a city creature neither by background nor by choice.

Niamh spent hours coaxing what she could from her companion. With prompting, Jenny complained at last of the machines which occupied the city by day, terrorised it by night. Of the noise they made, the smell. Of the bright lights which overwhelmed the joy of the evening, and the poisons which had dripped into the water. Where, had the pigs gone, the horses? What of London's famous bears? They had been the talk of the kingdom.

Jenny could not travel unaided beyond the bounds of the city. Not the modern city either, but the town she'd visited once, centuries before. The Thames was the southern border of her realm. To the west, she could go no further than the underground watercourse which had once been the famous River

Fleet. Escape the boundaries of the old city and Jenny's life became unbearable. A murderous coldness came upon her, burned like a fire through bracken. Her head sweltered. The world spun around her. Her throat choked. On the ground she lay, every breath a torment beyond words. Unless rain fell, unless its liquid pooled within reach of her fingers. Touch London water and she revived, the clouds gave way to light.

Determined to explore, Jenny had gone as far west as Lincoln's Inn Fields. She'd almost died with the effort. On another day, she'd travelled east as far as Shoreditch. A canal ledge near St John Street marked her furthest northern redoubt.

If she wasn't from London, and didn't choose the city, what force had brought her here? Jenny stared back at Niamh's question, her eyes the familiar twin pools of moonlight.

Niamh was standing at Tom Sanden's Holloway door. She struck the knocker against its plate, called out, "Courier." She heard him put down his newspaper. Uncertain steps approached the front door, paused behind it. "Signed-for delivery," Niamh said. He unlocked the front door placed it on the latch. He was a dark presence behind the door, blocking any light from the outside. "Sorry, mister," she said, "You'll need to open up." In her left hand, she held up a cardboard box. "It won't fit through."

"This isn't a good time," the old man grumbled, but he unlocked the door.

"Got to be signed for," she told him. "I'll need to come in, proof of delivery. The company's very particular, they must have everything accounted."

He stepped aside, let her push past him into the corridor, into his private space. It was, if anything, cosier than she'd expected. There must have been a Mrs Sanden once, because the carpet was thick beneath Niamh's feet and the armchair looked comfortable and over the settee someone, the former wife no doubt, had draped a tasselled rug.

"My parcel, please."

He stood in the way of her escape route. He looked older than she'd expected, thinner. He'd shaved that morning and there was a deep groove above his upper lip. As he looked at her, his eyes were alert, his mouth already curling in suspicion.

"I'm getting it," Niamh said. She placed the package on the table. She gave him the clipboard, the form. "There."

He said, "If you're a courier, where's your bike?"

"I parked it out the front."

"Where?"

"Out there." It was time for plan B. It needed her to sway a little, to look confused, and wretched. She said, "Look, I've got this condition. It's called Chronic Dehydration Disorder. My condition means I need to drink a glass of water, or I can't cope. I get dizzy, I collapse. You wouldn't want me fainting on your floor, would you?"

He didn't move.

She told him, "A glass of water, please. One glass and I'll leave, I promise."

Water for Jenny.

The man said. "Stay there – where I can see you."

There was a hatch to his right, an opening to the kitchen. Beyond it, she could see bowls, plates. In front of her, meanwhile, Tom Sanden's face was forming into resolve.

"Where's my water?"

In a loud, clear voice, he replied, "Leave now – or I'll call the police."

There was a grey phone in a docking station – closer to her

than him. With more confidence than she felt, Niamh said, "You wouldn't dare."

He moved faster than she'd expected, but not towards the phone. Instead, he reached through the hatch, into the kitchen. Then reaching back to face her, he raised a weapon. He waved it at her, held it at eye height. He said, "I've got this."

It was a small knife. Red, plastic. A blade, sort of.

"What're you going to do *with that* – peel a potato at me?"

For a moment, they glared at one another. The stupid old man with his little, blunt weapon. Her, waiting with her parcel.

Improvising, Niamh decided to try the truth. She said, "You're right, I'm not a courier. This box, here, if you open it, you'll find it holds two metres of bubble wrap. That's all. On the other hand, you must have worked out by now, I'm not used to sneaking my way into people's homes. I'm as scared of you as you are of me."

"I'm not frightened of you." The man stared at the peeler he was carrying. He said, "Perhaps I am, a little." Then to her, "If you've come for my savings–"

"I haven't."

"Good – because there aren't any."

"I believe you."

They stood there for a moment, the two antagonists watching each other, each calculating their next move.

She said, "Would you mind if I helped myself to a tea?"

The same hostile glare.

"I'll make you one too, if you tell me what you've got."

"Lemon and ginger," he said, shaking his head as if not believing his own weakness.

She went to the kitchen, poured the water. She felt a presence – the black dress.

"Give me a chance."

Words came whispering back, "*His ancestor.*"

"I'll do it."

When Niamh returned to the living area, her host had seated himself in the main armchair. She was pleased to see him accept the mug she offered. She was glad too, that he felt able to leave the peeler on the floor. He lifted the mug to his mouth. She feared she had made the tea too cold or too hot, had ruined it somehow.

"Not too weak?" she asked.

"Passable." Then, as if to answer a question she hadn't asked, he added, "I can't have caffeine after one o'clock, not at my age."

"Life's a bitch."

He looked at her again, "You were going to tell me what brought you to my house."

With a deep breath, Niamh began. "I know this is going to sound mad but bear with me, please. I've got a friend who's trying to find out anything she can about this ancestor of yours. He was in the North somewhere, four hundred years ago. I'm looking to see if any documents survived from that time."

Tom Sanden studied her.

Outside, the cars raged through the streets.

He said at last, "I hope you don't mind me saying this, but I find your generation inscrutable. It's as if society is saying that it's the role of the young to talk and the old to listen. That we're dinosaurs too feeble-minded to understand the information you're giving us. The words you speak, in isolation I understand them. Each individual phrase, I know what the words mean. The problem comes when I try to put them together. Because when I think again about what you've told me, it doesn't make any sense."

"Sorry. I've been telling the truth."

"Please don't say sorry. It's one of those awful words; it brings me out in a rash. Now start again from the beginning. You have a friend–"

"Yes."

"What is she? An antiques collector?"

"A historian."

"And she wants you to find out about my ancestors? Four centuries ago, you said, but, if this relative of mine goes back four centuries, that's thirteen generations. In one generation, I had two parents. In two generations, that's four grandparents. In thirteen generations, it's basic maths, that's eight thousand people."

"I went by your surname. There's two of you in Greater London, that's all."

"My dear, I'm not in the phone book."

"You're online," Niamh sighed. "You signed your MP's nomination forms."

"Not in this millennium."

"The old forms are still up there, if you know where to look."

"Marvellous," he said, "so that's how I'll be spending my dotage. With fraudsters knocking on my door because they've found my postcode somewhere on the world wide web." He drank some more tea. Then, he must have seen a slump in her shoulders because his voice softened. He said, "This ancestor, what was his name?"

"Edward Sanden."

He laughed. "The Chorley Troubadour? You must be joking." Then transformed with fresh, childlike enthusiasm he leapt to his feet. He reached into the shelves on the far wall, looked again. "Where is it?" He went to his desk, reached in a drawer, and took out a brown, leather-bound book. "Haven't looked at this in twenty years."

He unfolded his reading glasses.

Sanden navigated the pages. The tome was old, he cradled it like a child. He found at last the page he was looking for, "The morning flash'd with the warmth awake / For the dew had dissolv'd the sleep-thrall / and it seem'd as if by some sweet mistake / The stars had received an impromptu shake / and had caught on the boughs in their fall."

He smiled, as if looking for approval. He said, "A minor poet, I admit, and little talked about these days, but there's something gratifying nevertheless about having an ancestor who wrote. Even if he never went further than God and landscapes."

"Landscapes?"

"Flowers, trees, couldn't stand people. Didn't like them, we'd all let him down somehow. I would lend you my own copy, but it has a certain sentimental value, and it's no challenge to track down. They've got a copy in the British Library."

"He didn't have a problem with women?"

"Not that I've heard."

"But there must have been something, some grievance, the sort of thing that his neighbours would still be talking about it after he died?"

"Edward – and scandal? Not his style. He was a poet, a clerk, a gentleman farmer. He didn't shock anyone, he sat in his study and wrote."

As Niamh closed the front door, she thought of Jenny, remembering the suffering she had inflicted on Liam. Niamh whispered, "You'd better not harm him."

Jenny glared back, held Niamh long in her black cat's eyes. "Or-?"

Niamh stared back, "I'm saying – this one gets to live."

Jenny made as if to answer, gave an unwilling grunt. "As thou demand'st."

Behind her, Niamh breathed a low sigh of relief.

CHAPTER 8
HECTOR

Niamh was skipping class to spend her days with Jenny. She stretched her evenings out, keeping to a minimum any chance meetings with her landlady, any duty to explain where she'd been. Vron, thank goodness, was paying little attention to her. She was busy with pleasures of her own. She was going through a phase of reading detective fiction. She began with the golden age, the Agatha Christies and Josephine Tays sitting in a pile on her living room table, clock dials on their front covers, flower stems, a harlequin leering at his prey. Vron hid behind her bedroom door, reading as if the law forbade it. Downstairs, Tirzah and Rahab were waiting for Niamh. Greedy, servile, eyes stared at her from beneath the kitchen table. Until the last few weeks, Tirzah would not have permitted Niamh to stroke him. He ran through her legs rather than tolerate Niamh's kindness. When she tried to pick Tirzah up, he always scratched her with his back leg, clawed his way to freedom. Now, and as never before, he had cast away his former dignity. He flaunted his sides, begged to have her pet him.

After a time, Vron must have tired of her novels with their gentle perpetrators who killed by mistake, found themselves caught in traps of their own foolish making. A new set of books took over the living room. Stories set in derelict contemporary cities, with violent deaths in greater number. They lay half-finished on the table, crowded the floor.

"Do you want anything from the shop?" asked Niamh.

"We're out of olive oil," called Vron from behind her closed door.

The oil – being extra virgin, one litre, and *Italian, darling* – cost more than any treat Niamh had allowed herself in weeks.

In her dream that evening, Niamh found herself looking out from behind a stranger's eyes. She was in a building she didn't know, walking up a staircase she'd never seen before. She could see in front of her a pair of hands which weren't her own, male wrists, thick, with hairs jutting out from beyond white cuffs. When Niamh looked a second time, the hands remained, strange and unfamiliar. She fought the vision in front of her. Niamh twisted, made as if to compel herself to wake. She shouted out but no words came. The man – her *host* – was climbing up to a loft. Sofas, soft furnishings, thick Victorian brick walls, and sash windows. He was trying to close the windows at the far end of the room.

Then she smelled the old, familiar stink. Stagnant water, blood, rotting weeds. She heard someone whispering *Niamh*. The word crackled in her ears.

Why did you bring me, without any warning? Niamh answered, making her voice as sharp as she could. *We spent the morning together. You didn't need to kidnap me*.

Her throat tightened, as if an unseen power had placed a hand over her mouth. Niamh tried to speak, again without success. Twisted her body without moving.

Hush, child, the voice answered. *Tis how it must be.*

She tried to wriggle, but iron bounds held her neck and chest. She tried in vain to slow her heart, soften the brutal pressure on her chest.

In front of the man, the windows were on a slant, water poured in through them. Again, Niamh struggled against the prison in which Jenny had trapped her. The man closed one window frame, slammed another shut. "I don't need this," he said.

I want to go home, Niamh whispered, hoping with all her strength that Jenny was listening, would do as she asked.

Home, she begged.

The rain battered the glass, loud and hostile. She'd never heard nature rage like this. The windows wavered beneath the water's assault. Niamh could feel fear rising in the man's heart, the muscles squirming inside his chest, squeezing him, squeezing her. His breath was accelerating, as was hers inside him. He grabbed at the rug, which was now sodden, the ruined cushions. "What the hell?" He tramped back down the ladder, paused as he listened to the rain drilling at the house, the water invading from all sides. A woman looked up from the bed. She had a stud in her nose, a smear of red henna in her hair. Niamh had spent so many nights dreaming of Jenny's adventures. She knew what to expect. The man would shake his companion; he'd order her out of bed and reveal himself to be a brute.

Tonight, though, the man's voice was gentle. He said, "Chickpea, do you mind?"

"Mind what?"

"Getting up."

The rain thundered down in great sleety pebbles. The man went to the bathroom. Here, too, the windows were open. As he approached, something grazed his knuckle. The pain was so sharp, it was as if the ice had pierced Niamh's own skin. His hand was red. He swore, slammed the window shut, bought himself a moment of peace. Still the rain lashed down, picked at the window frame, tried to force its way in. He rinsed the hand in warm water. He looked up at the mirror. Niamh studied him, the three-day stubble, the night-shirt, a hint of blue at the edge of his glasses. His chin, there was something about his chin.

Let him go, Niamh urged. *What did he do to harm you?*

Doubt me not, child. The words sounded in Niamh's ear like a whisper travelling over water. Niamh twisted to look and see if Jenny was inside the room. Where was she?

The man rubbed the wounded area on a hand towel. He looked for a clock. 03:30 the display said. He turned at the sound of the rain pressing on the windows in the hallway. "The world's gone mad," he said. He left the room.

Back into the corridor he went. Niamh too – wondering if she'd seen him or when.

Niamh knew what water in the sink meant. All it needed was an inch of liquid, unmoving, stagnant, and there would be Jenny – as if he had invited her into his home. Niamh tried to warn him. Urged him to go back.

The man stood in the corridor, paused at a closed door, listening to the rough-and-tumble sounds of a child sleeping. *Don't do this*, she begged.

He returned to the bedroom. His companion had gone back to sleep. The man knelt by her, said, "You need to get up. Please. Something's wrong outside."

"What's wrong?"

"I can't explain, you need to see it for yourself."

"I'm tired," she said.

"Please, can't you take a look – for my sake?"

Niamh waited for the man to curse, to say it was the woman's fault. To complaining that she was nagging him. The conflict which would give Jenny an excuse.

What the man said was, "The rain, it's too much. I can't explain it – there's something weird out there. It's not normal. It shouldn't be like this."

Niamh wished that her companion would find a lesser

punishment suitable for a lesser crime. *You don't need to ruin his life, for being an average guy.*

"You've woken me up for rain?"

"It's more than rain. What sleet can do that?"

Niamh heard the rain charge, felt the glass quiver at each attack. "There's a plaster in the cupboard," the woman said. Her voice was so soft, it made Niamh's heart break.

The man looked down, saw the small towel still wrapped around it. He stood there as she rose, removed the material that surrounded it, dressed it a second time. "The storm," he said, in a weak voice. "That's what I keep on saying. There's something screwed about the weather. We've never had weather like this in London."

The woman had pulled herself up. "Ok, ok."

"I need you to tell me I'm not going crazy."

"You'd better not be." A tired smile.

Again, the rain fell – stone chipping against glass.

Niamh said, *We can get the information without torturing the guy. Whatever you want from him, I can find it another way.*

Too late, Jenny answered.

The man took the floor below, checked that the windows were holding on against the intrusion from outside. He looked in the dining room, placed his good hand on the old wooden frames, paused to listen to the wind between the rain, the gusting of the trees outside, the eager, insistent beating of the wind upon the glass.

Niamh caught his reflection a second time in the mirror. She had seen him before. She'd swear to it, but where?

The man returned to the first floor of the house – to the bathroom, to their bedroom, to a closed door. Listened for the sound of someone sleeping beyond it. The woman joined him. The man was staring through the window. He said, "It's getting worse."

"Can't we go back to bed? We've done all we can."

"I need a drink," he said.

"Hector–" the woman answered.

Niamh squeezed her fists into a useless ball, screamed a silent scream. Hector. It all made sense now, Hector Sanden. The second man with that surname in London. Tom's younger brother. That's why she'd recognised him. The little cleft above his lips, under his thin moustache. She could see the similarity with Tom, although Tom was older. Hector, of course. Niamh had found his address online. Given it to Jenny. Made herself complicit.

I never asked for this.

No answer.

She started to beg. *Let me go back, I was sleeping, I don't want anything to do with this. I never agreed. You never warned me it would be like this.* Shouting the words, she cried out, *I was asleep for Christ's sake! You should have left me there.*

Thou dost protest like a priest.

Hector went downstairs to their sitting room. Lifting two neglected glasses, he let them clink together as if the louder the sound the better the chance of ignoring the storm outside.

"Macallan 1947," he said, reaching into a wooden cabinet, lifting a bottle, and holding it with great care. "My red, red rose," he recited, "sprung anew in June."

The woman had followed him, "There's soda in the fridge."

"Soda, with this belle dame sans merci?"

Hector came back from the kitchen, bringing two whisky glasses, and a jar of ice, but no soda. As he returned to the sitting room, with its large windows, the sound of the rain caused his pulse to quicken. It was more insistent than ever.

He put down the glasses. He stared.

There was a crash, like a brick forcing itself in through the glass. Hector recoiled, as if someone had directed the attack at him. Recovering, he went to investigate. It wasn't a brick, it was a splinter of ice which had broken through the window, landed on the floor.

The woman said. "I'll get the dustpan."

Hector ignored her, his eyes scanning the floor for the splinter. He bent down, reached for it. He grabbed the object. It was white, hard as a stalactite. Cold enough to burn. "Shit," he cried out, dropping it to the floor. "*Ow*."

There was the smell again – damp, dust, and decay.

The woman returned, swept the shard into a pan. "What even was that?"

A second shot came from outside, broke another pane of glass. A third. With each assault, Hector's legs buckled.

A sound of crying came from upstairs.

"Simeon," the woman said.

He didn't wait for her. Hector raced upwards, his chest tight, stretching with each step, taking the stairs two, three, at a time.

Niamh was running with him. *If you touch the man–*

Wouldst thou disown our compact?

Hector scrambled for the switch, but no light came. He heard a child crying out. "Sims?" he said. As Hector stumbled into the room, the night was cold, the dark swirling around him. "Dad's here," Hector said, grabbing the child into his arms. Through the windows, ice pellets struck against his body. The missiles ricocheted off his skin.

Hector's whole body was raging with a desperate urge to protect. Niamh felt the boy's heartbeat answering, the great loosening as the child hugged his father back.

"Come to Mummy," the woman said. She carried the boy

out through the door.

Hector sobbed in relief. "Our Father," he mumbled, "which art in Heaven–" Great lumps of ice came at his face. He turned his face away, trying to protect his eyes as he heaved at the window frame. "Thy will be done–" he gabbled. Niamh felt the ice-shards as they searched for Hector's hands, his head. His eyes. "Forgive us our trespass-es–" Hector crashed the window shut. He sank down against the wall. She could hear his son crying in the distance. The assault of the rain, the sleet subsided for a moment.

Hector waited for his breathing to slow. "For ever, and ever. *Amen.*" Niamh felt his mind sink inwards. The desper-ate beating of his heart. "Amen," he said.

She told Jenny, *I needed someone to help me. I didn't choose this.*

The man checked himself for injuries. He closed his eyes, prepared to stand.

"Hector?" a voice came from the distance. The wife. "Talk to me."

"I'm fine," he told her. Then, in a quieter voice, "What the hell?"

He could hear the tread of feet approaching.

Hector shrank down as the figure towered over him. The black dress. Fear shook through Hector, made his skin burn with helpless rage. He looked at the creature, his body shud-dering with fantasies of revenge. "What kind of monster are you?"

"Thine own ancestor's beloved friend. The temptation that resisted him," Jenny answered. Then, down she reached her hands, caressing them around his neck.

She twisted, *hard*. The movement sundered his flesh, the delicate bones of his neck. To Niamh's surprise, Hector did not cry out in pain. Nor was his neck sore. It was warm rather, the warm woozy sensation of liquid out of place.

"Hector?" his wife shouted. "What's going on?"

His legs slid out beneath him.

Hector's chest – Niamh's chest – was spasming. She begged Jenny, *Let me go*. Niamh howled the words in a desperate fury.

"The door," the wife sobbed, "Why did you lock it?"

Little cells danced in front of Hector's eyes.

Oh shit, Niamh thought. *Oh shit, oh shit, oh shit –*

Niamh could still sense Jenny, the dampness of her black dress, the familiar stink of piss and rotting weeds that Jenny always carried with her.

You can't, Niamh thought. *It's all wrong. It's–*

Hector's sight had gone. A twitch of blood, and the man was somewhere else. A house. A clearing. The building, its walls painted white, its brick chimney, the slant of its red tile roof. A lake at its side, the sound of frogs singing from the reeds. A smile formed. He'd been happy there. Fifty panes of glass on each floor. The house in which he'd been born.

With the last throb of blood in the man's ears, Niamh saw a face. Pale with lines so deep it was as if his maker had carved them in wax. The look as he bent down to face a younger Hector was kind, solicitous even, and yet beneath his smile, there was a cruel fierceness.

Edward, Jenny said, her voice rich with satisfaction. *I was not wrong.*

Niamh felt Hector's body slacken. She felt his relief as the last sounds trickled away. The pain had gone. Niamh would not have called these last moments unpleasant. They were the rectification of a mistake, the final loosening of a knotted string.

Sick with fear, Niamh waited. She hadn't done anything to harm Jenny – now here she was, about to die alongside him.

Why, she asked, *what crime could justify that?*

No answer came. Instead, the night was quiet. It was dark; it was still. Until at last, as if she were a forgotten memory, her body convulsed.

She was back in her bed, at home. Her chest quivering without control.

CHAPTER 9
HEALING TIME

Three weeks passed. Niamh was hiding in Vron's maisonette. She was grateful for the bronze figures on the mantelpiece of her landlady's front room, the orchid in the vase, the wax model of a woman's torso. Soon, it would be a month without Jenny and Niamh was delighted. She was finding it easier to pretend that her life had never parted from its normal course. She returned to class, meant to go. She was going back, was about to leave – she would have done by now if it wasn't for Aitch and Jake. Her life shrank to her landlady, the flat, the streets outside. Vron had noticed that Niamh was in the house more. She had spent a week sulking, but that period of grizzling was over. Vron was talkative again, brittle, intrusive. Splendid in her first-cocktail-at-six everyday routine. That was what Niamh needed now, a life without shocks or surprises. For twenty-one days, she'd given up swimming in the wild water of the reservoir abandoned even the swimming pool, taken up yoga instead, finding solace in the earthy realism of Cat, Cow, and Downward Dog (best to forget her sharp intake of breath at Boat pose, her desperate fidgeting in Corpse). She kept a distance between her and the canal. Niamh waited until Vron had left, then went round the bathroom drying every surface.

Pimlico was south of Westminster, beyond the furthest reach of King James's London, beyond the reach of Jenny's power. That said, Niamh still took precautions. Every time she walked past the bathroom, she tightened the taps. The kitchen taps, too. Those steps would not keep Jenny at a distance forever, but, for the moment, Niamh felt safe – more or less.

Vron meanwhile, was in as good a mood as any that Niamh could remember. She'd adopted a middle-aged beau, Dominic – Valentino blazer, brass buttons, apollo curls.

He and Vron were due to go out that evening to play backgammon. Dominic couldn't understand why Vron always beat him. With a rueful smile, he insisted that she must have cheated, that Vron rolled the dice in a way which was contrary to all the laws of logic. Niamh liked the idea of Vron cheating. It would fit with other aspects of her landlady's personality – her need for admiration, Vron's insistence that life had been cruel to her, a harshness which entitled her to do whatever she liked in response. There was something gratifying about imagining her landlady attending these occasions with loaded dice, a pair of sixes concealed beneath the wrists of her cashmere rollneck.

That evening, Tirzah approached, wary of Rahab's aggression. He offered himself to Niamh, purring in a tone of look-at-us-both-creatures-together desperation.

Dominic meanwhile was Pimm's and lime juice woozy. As cheery as the meal ahead of him. He was singing Niamh's praises, "A right little scholar you've got, I bet she keeps you up every evening chatting with her boffin friends."

"It's Vron who's the night owl," Niamh said, beaming at her landlady.

"Nonsense, darling," said Vron.

"Look at this." Dominic took an old book out of his Harrods bag, showed it to Vron, then showed it to Niamh. "What do you reckon?"

"It's nice," Niamh told him. The volume was old, bound in calfskin which had aged, and turned jet-black. There was something pleasing about the book, how it weighed heavy in her hand. She turned to the inside page. The Life and Strange Surprising Adventures of *Robinson Crusoe*. She found the date – 1719. She let out a little grunt of enthusiasm.

"What's the damage?" he asked.

"I'm sorry, I don't know."

"Don't be one of them," her landlady answered.

"One of what?"

"Those awful young people who won't do anything to help."

Niamh looked back at her landlady. "But–"

"Don't worry," Dominic said. "It's no biggie."

"What would he get for it?" Vron demanded. "That's all he's asking."

"How come he's asking me?"

"Can't you look it up?"

Vron turned back to Dominic. "The youth of today, it's not fair, they never suffered. They've never gone without. Everything comes to them – mobile phones, 24-hour delivery. They don't know what it was like. When I was born, I was part of a generation that–"

"Fought in the war?" asked Niamh.

"No, but our parents had, and our teachers had. They were all Corporal this, and Chief Women's Officer that. We showed our elders due respect."

"Give the poor girl a chance," Dominic said. "Niamh doesn't need the two of us wittering on about how good things used to be." He smiled at Vron, then winked at Niamh as if the few years which separated him from Vron made him Niamh's co-conspirator.

Niamh gave the book back to Dominic. Said, "I'd love to help but it's beyond me."

"It's history," Vron said.

Niamh stared into her mug, a teabag that she'd microwaved in milk, before answering. She had met history, conspired with history, had kept her silence when history went on a murderous rampage against a series of men, several of whom but not all had deserved it. What doofus would introduce themselves to the past when they should be running as fast as they could away from it in the opposite direction?

"I'm sorry," she said. "I don't mean to be difficult, but I wouldn't know where to start."

"You're an ungrateful minx," said Vron.

"I'm sorry," Niamh said.

Dominic was good for Vron. When she went upstairs to her room, Niamh could hear Vron and Dominic giggling at the start of the blue-ray he'd rented. You'd think it was some teenage party and Niamh was the parent; she'd be the one who'd wake up the next morning, hear the two conspirators rushing to tidy up before Niamh caught them.

On mornings like that, Vron had such an expression of joy on her face, it was obscene. She'd say things like, "He's very energetic, Dominic."

"Is he?" Niamh said. "I don't need to know."

Seeing Vron happy with Dominic made Niamh think of Liam. If he'd had more time, he would have come back to her. He'd have taken Niamh to the cinema, and they'd have seen two dozen films by now. They'd have eaten every cuisine in London, even the obscure ones: Bolivian, Eritrean. There was another version of their lives in which Liam and Niamh were both still doing their History course, both coming back in the evenings, listening to CDs, playing Risk with their friends. No, not Risk, Aitch would be a nightmare at Risk. She'd garrison all her armies in Australia, wait till everyone else had fought themselves to a standstill, then send her tanks sneaking north and west. While, as for Jake, he'd have conquered Asia in round one – and held it ever since, leaving

Liam raging against him.

This was the best there was to say about Niamh's life, the joy of joys, the one thing that counted as "good." For three weeks, she hadn't seen anything of the water creature. Her future had taken a different direction from the past. She was in some new state – bail, or parole, call it what you like – and she was doing her best to stay there.

Another week passed. Then a note came from Niamh's sister. When Niamh told her landlady that Yvonne would be in London, Vron smiled a benevolent smile, said, "Let's take her out." A new bistro had opened, it was a cereal shop in the morning, did cakes in the afternoon, and for dinner they served mackerel and stewed kumquats. Niamh hadn't had the heart to answer, *I'll go. I'll go anywhere you like, but if you think Yvonne's coming with us, she won't. She'll find something better, or she'll cancel at the last minute. She always does.*

Dance. That had once been a new beginning. All Niamh had needed to do was stand there, bend her knees, stretch her arms up, never forgetting her dad in the car outside or Yvonne grumbling how the house was cold without them. The teacher said, "She'll be tall, that one, like Audrey Hepburn." Over the rest of that first class, Niamh had been her dance class's Anna Pavlova, its Carmen Amaya. She had a future in not eating if the teacher's stares spoke true. That first class had been the best. She was going to be a star. The lessons had also been, from a longer perspective, a *valuable learning experience.* For, after those first few weeks of glory, dance had sunk. Into the second week, it was still all praise. *La fille, elle est mignonne,* but there was a smell behind them, an antiseptic odour of looming disappointment. Niamh knew what local gossips said about the teacher, Madame Mille-Feuille

– the vodka in her thermos, not the good stuff, not Smirnoff, not Botanical Vodka nor Absolut Watermelon, but winos' delight. The sort of drink that would strike like a bucket of ice to the face, float your hair, crinkle your toes. So, when the teacher had put Niamh in *Mermaids*, promoted her to *Dames at Sea*, then again to *Anything Goes*, it had been all false hopes, all of it a betrayal.

It was Yvonne who prophesised Niamh's fall. Too old to start dance at the age of eleven, she'd been big enough to be jealous and to demand some balancing kindness to match the money they were lavishing on Niamh's dance lessons. Their dad had looked around Yvonne's room, thought, and offered to buy her a classical guitar. An electric guitar, Yvonne said.

Niamh and her dad drove into central Birmingham for the lessons, walked up the hill. New Street. Madame Mille-Feuille, cheques made out to Doris Kelly please, had left Niamh as the teacher stranded her in *Anything Goes*, returned her to *Dames*, then a fortnight later sent her sliding all the way back down to *Mermaids*.

"Serves you right," Yvonne had said. Then returned to her room and played a triumphant solo on her new-bought guitar, amp and flanger pedal.

You couldn't fight Yvonne, she always won.

Niamh's sister was now in her last year of uni. She had her own house, and no need to see her younger sister. Wouldn't have come to London, if it hadn't been for her agent who'd booked her band a week of happenings at every pub along Upper Street.

Niamh was in bed staring at the flyer that her sister had posted her. An advertisement for a gig, on top of which Yvonne had written in biro, "We can go for a meal after."

Being literal, which was always wise when you had

Yvonne as a sister, Niamh could not see a direct invitation to the concert. To the meal afterwards, yes, but not to the performance. Niamh texted, "Can I bring a friend?"

Niamh looked again at the flyer, at the image of her sister's band, with Yvonne's boyfriend and bassist Florence in his black-and-cherry shirt, his long hair, and beard. The red stage curtains behind them. *Don't mess this up.*

When Dominic arrived, Vron was upstairs, putting her face on.

He asked Niamh, "Are you looking forward to the show?"

"The show?"

"Your sister's band. Vron told me all about it. Said we were all invited."

Niamh smiled, but inside she was screaming. One friend she'd mentioned, but now the plan had extended to two. And two wrinklies, at that. Yvonne would record the names of Niamh's guests in the great sororal desk diary as proof of Niamh's selfishness, her incompetence, her dogged insistence on ruining everything Yvonne did.

"I'm so glad you can make it," Niamh said. "It's years since I've seen them." It seemed a sturdier answer than the alternative which would have been to explain that Yvonne had never invited Niamh to hear any of her bands before, had always banned her, and the chances were that Niamh's control-freak of a sister wouldn't say hi to her all evening.

"And you're a musician, too, if I remember," said Dominic, smiling at himself for having dredged up the fact from the drowned banks of his memory.

"I had lessons when I was a kid," Niamh answered, meaning the dance.

"You've kept it up?"

"I try," answered Niamh, feeling the flush on her cheeks which happened every time she lied. "But it's been so difficult, you know, with the course, and everything."

Dominic nodded.

A gust of wind must have caught the tree outside, as there was a brief flurry of water on the window-pane. Niamh closed her eyes, breathed in and out.

Dominic said, "Any chance of some water?"

"We're out of it," Niamh told him. Then realising how strange that must have sounded, she went on, "I broke the tap, I'm afraid, but if you'd like a brandy?"

"Why not?" said Dominic. "Maybe in a bit."

Niamh could feel the back of her neck redden, as if it was summer already, the height of summer, and she'd spent the full day sunbathing.

Dominic opened his jacket, and, with a conspiratorial flourish, revealed the packet of polos he'd hidden there. "Look what I've packed," he told her.

Niamh smiled a ragged smile.

"You'll understand in a few years. Go to a concert, and it's the hardest thing staying awake. A pack of these, mind you, and you'll stay up through anything."

Niamh was processing that word, *concert*. "Dominic," she said, "Vron did warn you, didn't she, that Yvonne's band are quite loud?"

Dominic shrugged. "I've listened to Wellington's Victory," he said, "and that had cannons. I've been to see U2, Dire Straits. I'm not some fogey for you to laugh at."

At last, Vron had finished, and came downstairs to rescue Niamh.

"Gosh," said Dominic, jumping to his feet. "Look at you." Then, with a bow, he said, "With a dress like that, you could sink a thousand ships." He reached his lips towards Vron's face. She stood on tiptoe to accept his kiss. He handed her a box of Charbonnel et Walker.

Niamh was torn between relief and guilt. She hadn't yet mentioned that Yvonne hadn't invited the others, but she'd have to tell them soon enough.

Dominic and Vron were looking at each other, inching closer to one another as if they were about to kiss and the presence of Niamh in the room must have had some effect in cooling their mutual ardour, since Dominic took a step backwards. Then reaching forward again, he pinched Vron once on the arms. He grinned liked a child.

"Incorrigible," said Vron, in a do-it-again voice.

Yvonne's band were every bit as noisy as Niamh had hoped, then noisier still, with an extra layer of volume reserved for those people who might have been complaining that there wasn't much need to turn the amps up to thirteen in such a small basement. They reminded Niamh of the Birmingham of her youth, when all the songs in the jukeboxes had been Black Sabbath or Judas Priest. At High School, the bands had names like Satanic Sixpence, Nuclear Beast. In Memoriam. The boys with their greasy black hair.

By contrast to them, Yvonne's band-mate Florence was the very incarnation of changing tastes. Florence smelled of vanilla pods. He wore a dress beneath his clean locks, his immaculate beard. There was a distinct rural tone to his songs. A boy mourned his father who was away working. An old man worked in the fields, in honour of his dead son. The songs were tight. Niamh could believe in the words. They had an audience, too, all the goth boys and goth girls from Camden Lock, from the Unicorn.

It would have been perfect, but for the condensation streaming down the walls. Niamh shivered. *No*, she was thinking. *Don't you dare*.

Niamh looked up and saw Vron beaming at her.

When the event was over, Niamh said they should all go to the mackerel restaurant. To Niamh's surprise, Yvonne and Florence agreed.

They arrived at the diner, which didn't seem to be much more than a few tables propped against a wall. Vron ordered the house special. Niamh chose the most sensible choice, lentil dal. She listened while Vron told the waiter how brilliant Yvonne and Florence had been.

The waiter asked about drinks.

"Tap water for the table," Dominic said.

"Let's not," Niamh answered. "Let's get a bottle of white. I'll pay – my loan came in." She checked around the others, and no one objected.

"Do you go to gigs often?" Vron asked the waiter, playing the role of surrogate mum. Any moment now, she'd say, *They're so talented, I don't know where they get it from.*

Looking from musician to musician, Vron said, "You've got so much potential."

The way to impress Vron, it turned out, was to tell her about the other bands they'd played with; how the musicians in those other, lesser, acts had performed at Reading or at Glastonbury or opened for people who Vron had seen on TV.

The restaurant didn't serve alcohol. Niamh helped Dominic as he went to the off-license next door, then ordered a small truckload of drink. While they were queuing to pay, Dominic said, "Course they aren't real musicians."

"Aren't they?" Niamh asked.

Dominic started to answer, stopped. When he started again, his face was white. "Niamh," he said, "would you mind if I asked your advice?"

"Sure."

"I've been thinking about popping the question."

For an awful moment, Niamh thought Dominic was talking of proposing to her. Then, she realised, and had to stifle a laugh of disbelief. “Marry her?”

“You don’t think it’s too soon, do you?”

“I don’t know,” said Niamh. “Are you sure it’s a wise idea? I mean, I’m not at all sure she’s got over Quentin.” As Niamh looked up and saw the expression on Dominic’s face, she hated herself for saying it. “It’s difficult,” she said, “when there are children involved.” But was that true? Did they still count as children when they were in their thirties?

“You’re right,” Dominic said. “No good to go in all guns blazing. Discretion the better part of valour, and all that.”

God, Niamh was thinking, *and now I’ve ruined everything for him, too.*

When they returned to the restaurant, Vron’s gleaming happiness,” You’re so professional, you should go on Top of the Pops,” was wearing down even Yvonne’s extraordinary ability to absorb praise. Her sister at last looked in Niamh’s direction.

Niamh took the movement as her cue. She said, “Come on, sis, let’s talk.”

“What’s wrong?”

“I’ve missed you,” she said. For a moment, she was willing to forget everything, her sister’s self-satisfaction, the brittle dryness of her bleached hair – Niamh was a natural blonde, for years she’d resented Yvonne for copying her – her perfect complexion.

“It’s been a while,” Yvonne said.

Niamh said, “But I’m glad I got out.” Then because her sister’s face was blank, she said. “Fled the nest. Escaped from the Planet of the Apes.”

It had been the theme of their childhood. Yvonne had permission to leave; she was going to get married. When Yvonne settled down, it was going to be anywhere at all, outside Britain if that was where her work took her. But Niamh, as the youngest, had a duty to stay home. Niamh would nurse their mum (nearly fifty, already a veteran hypochondriac) through old age. Niamh. Unless her mum found the hunky Spanish waiter that she'd always talked about. No one had ever planned as far into the future as the part where Niamh had the chance of going to uni. If they had, the implication would have been obvious. She could study in Birmingham. She could spend her days at the course, her evenings at home. Escaping her mum's plans had been Niamh's greatest achievement.

"London's great," Niamh continued, speaking the words as much for her own benefit as for her sister. "The clubs, the bars, I'm out every evening."

Yvonne said, "That's wonderful, Neevie. My little sister, growing up at last."

"And I've got a boyfriend, too."

"What's he like?" Yvonne asked.

Niamh took a quick look to check that Vron wasn't eavesdropping. Her landlady was deep in conversation with Dom. He's kind," Niamh said, "brains too, handsome. You look at him and think he's going bald, but he isn't, that's how he likes it." *How Liam liked it.*

"So, what's the catch?"

"No catch," answered Niamh. "And he's got great taste in music."

"Yeah?"

"Indie music. Words you can hear, songs like stories."

"So where is this well-informed dreamboat?"

"I'll introduce you. He wanted to be here, he's caught up in something." Niamh groaned inside as her cheeks reddened.

Yvonne turned to Florence. "You get this? My sister the escape artist, and she's found herself the horniest young stud."

"Give me his number," said Florence.

Yvonne laughed. She pulled Florence closer, kissed him, bit him on the cheek.

Something about these movements must have disturbed Dominic because he stopped in the middle of the anecdote he was telling, in which a cricketer was – was what? Vron would never know – because something about Florence and Yvonne's intimacy seemed to disturb him. He snorted, sped his way in tortured silence through the rest of the meal.

Niamh still felt she had unfinished business with her sister. So, when Dominic offered to drive Vron and Niamh home, which he did not long after, Niamh said she'd rather walk.

Vron and Dominic waved their goodbyes.

Yvonne said, "Can I have a water?"

"No," Niamh said. "We've had all the drinks we need. The bill, please."

The waiter looked at Yvonne, Yvonne looked at Florence.

"The bill."

"There's nothing wrong, is there?" Yvonne said.

"I've never been better," lied Niamh.

Silence surrounded them.

It seemed to Niamh that if she didn't say something now it would be months, years even, before she had a chance again. She said, "You're not annoyed with me, are you?"

"Why would I be angry?"

"I don't know – for foisting the wrinklies on you."

"They were a hoot," said Florence.

Yvonne had put a hand on her boyfriend's wrist. She told him, "Give us five minutes."

Florence made to protest, but he saw the look on Yvonne's face. "Sure, doll."

After he'd left, Yvonne said, "Tell me then, why should I

be annoyed with you?"

"I've got a favour to ask. When you go back to Aberdeen, can I come with you? Let me stay in your flat. I'll get a job. Help me out till I've got some money coming in, that's all I'm asking. I can cook, I can clean. It'd be the two us against the world."

"What about your degree?"

"It's fine – people defer all the time." Yvonne gave an equivocal smile. Taking heart, Niamh said, "So you don't mind if I come back with you?"

Yvonne said, "I'll talk to Florence."

"All right," said Niamh. "Thank you." She added, "But don't fob me off. I couldn't cope if I thought you were ignoring me."

"Jesus," Yvonne said. "I told you I'd ask, didn't I?"

"You'll do what you can?"

"I will," Yvonne told her, raising a hand in warning. Enough.

Niamh said, "Don't pass me around like a parcel. There's no law which means you've got to ask Florence first."

Yvonne pulled herself up in her chair. If, before, there'd been a drunken, tipsy look about her face, now her eyes were stone-cold sober. "That's quite a way of putting it."

"Please. I need to get out of here," Niamh said.

"Why?"

Niamh winced. Excited as she was after the evening and even with a glass of wine inside her, she wasn't going to say, *because a psychotic water creature is chasing me*. Instead, she replied, "You need to trust me on this. I need a break from London – that's all."

"Are you up the duff?"

"No."

"Then what?" said Yvonne.

"Why won't you take me?"

Yvonne said, "We've been through this before, haven't we?"

"You haven't spoken to me in two years."

Yvonne was in full flow now, "We spoke a year ago. Eighteen months ago, and you tried the same move on me then. Kid, you may not remember but I do. The answer is the same as it was then. I don't want you following me around like you did at school."

"That's harsh."

"What about Joseph Oliver?"

Niamh closed her eyes. She tried to remember. These were the facts. Joseph Oliver had been a friend of Yvonne's. He'd come back to their house once, twice at the utmost. One of those times, he'd knocked on Niamh's door and reached in to kiss her, reached his hand beneath her top.

Niamh said, with as much dignity as she could muster, "He made me." The words sat in the air between the two sisters.

"He *made you*?"

"Please," begged Niamh, her heart looping, and swirling. "I need to leave the city."

"He *made you* act like a slut?"

"That's not right," Niamh said. "I tried to push him away and, after that, you blanked me. The whole way through GCSEs, you wouldn't even look at me, let alone talk to me when I needed it – and why? Because I'd ruined your chances with Joseph Oliver? He had a brace. He couldn't stop banging on about Star Trek, and you cared more about him than me."

Yvonne scowled at her. "He'd got rid of the brace by the summer."

"Please," Niamh begged. "I'm not safe here." She winced, hated the words as she spoke them. "I won't go back to Birmingham. You're my one chance of a home life."

Yvonne looked at Niamh. She said, “If you can’t hack it on your stupid course–”

“Then what?”

“Then you’ll have to lump it,” Yvonne said. “You can’t keep on begging me to rescue you. We die on our own, kid, that’s how life is. The sooner you learn, the better.”

CHAPTER 10
HOPE

Niamh's dreams began again, as unsettling as they'd been before. In one, there was a man – she'd seen him on YouTube, he had hair out of the 1970s, a born-again Mark Bolan. He liked to burn his girlfriends. He couldn't arouse himself without a lighter in his right hand. He liked to roll the wheel with his thumb, feel the gratifying heat as it singed his callused flesh. He caressed his gifts, worshipped the brown spots he left behind. The star was a great believer in consent, made a point of obtaining written permission before the evening's start. It was so hard to predict those difficult types, the skirt who said they agreed then made a fuss afterwards. Make them sign a contract, though, and you could get a court order. Not that there was any need to bother the law. After they signed, the women silenced themselves. When the social media celebrity quit his hotel-room that evening, he saw a heap of clothes, discarded at the canal-side. He thought they were abandoned rags until they shifted, revealing a woman in distress. She demanded his help, and the man bent down towards her, playing in real-life his favourite screen role – a doctor. He asked if anything was wrong. He offered to call an ambulance. As he peered at the woman in her shabby black dress, she came to life. The man begged for mercy, tried to offer money. She flicked her shoulders, threw him into the water. Dived in after him. Became a struggling rage of fury. She pulled him down into the darkness.

The students were supposed to be choosing the topics for

their dissertations. When Niamh had begun the course, she'd had the idea of filling in the missing chapters in *Malone's History*, reflecting how the past had been understood then and what readers cared about now. She'd write the necessary sections on women, on children, on sex, on the transformation of the countryside which made possible the rise of industry, of the shrinking of the working week, of the determination to save the environment. All of this would prove that the past was making the present, was creating the conditions for a better world. But the images Jenny had shown her, they made it even harder to believe in that liveable future.

Niamh walked up the entrance stairs of the British Library. She had decided to write a case study of the northern gentry. She read Edward Sanden's poems. She could imagine the gritstone fells, the heather waving "neath blowing zephyrs," the drystone walls. She'd studied the historians as they debated which King had shown him the greater favour, James or Charles. His descendants had occupied Sanden Hall for four centuries. A cousin had served in the Parliamentary armies, fought at Naseby. Travelling the roads at much the same time had been Matthew Hale, the lawyer. She imagined the two of them, the King's prosecutor meeting the Lancashire laureate, bonding over their shared anger at the unjust grumblings of the poor, of women. The men were the spirit of commerce, the architects of the present.

The 1600s, she believed, were a turning point in history. This, the Salt Professor had taught her: we date the temperature of the world from that time. When we say that it is already 1.5 degrees hotter than it used to be, we have as our baseline the start of the sixteenth century. The date marked the greatest extent of the Amazon forest, the time after the arrival of Columbus, after the plagues he'd brought had killed fifty million Native Americans, after the trees had grown over their abandoned corpses. Never again would there be so much nature drawing carbon from the sky. It was during these years that Galileo had published his *Sidereus Nuncius*, showing the stars orbiting Jupiter, dethroning the earth from the centre of the universe. In England, too, people's sense of themselves had changed. While Sanden was painting his landscapes in words, on Salisbury Plain Charles I was ordering the first archaeological dig at Stonehenge. The Duke of Buckingham dug up the silt covering the monument. His men found a complete altar stone, abandoned human bones, suits of armour eaten up by rust. Then for the first time historians had realised, as Malone put it, that the stones had stood there *when the Giants lived, when Albine's children had danced.*

Niamh was hoping a good mark in her dissertation might excuse her long weeks of absence but the more she planned her study of the Sandens, the worse were the doubts she felt. Two months had passed since she'd met Jenny. For half of that time, Niamh had gone to sleep, and her dreams had been her own and had ended without suffering. She woke with plans of fleeing London, abandoning her degree, settling somewhere far away. She dragged herself around the maisonette plotting her departure. By mid-morning she would be thinking about Edward Sanden once more, wondering if some fresh approach would reveal the reasons for Jenny's hatred, if there was a clue in his poems, in the essays of his modern-day critics.

All these thoughts, their reformulations and negations were warring in Niamh's head as she sat upon a bench, the library buildings towering behind her.

She saw a familiar figure walking towards her. Jake. She must have noticed him before he saw her, because she saw him give a startled jump, then shine his bashful smile.

"Hey, stranger," he said. "I didn't think you'd be here. Have you got a minute?"

She didn't want him there, hadn't forgiven him, but she looked again at the boy with his long hair over his ears, and he made her think of Dougal from the Magic Roundabout. She couldn't be cross with a kid who looked like that

He sat down; said, "I miss how things were."

"It's not my fault they changed." As soon as Niamh had said that she winced inside. Because it was her fault, wasn't it? All of it.

He said, "Is it true you took Liam's watch?"

The directness of his question surprised her. *How dare you*? she'd should have said, but the June sun was warm. It was no day for anger.

She told him, "That friend of yours, she gave it to me, and if you don't believe me, I'm telling you – I'll throw you in the canal."

"It's ok, I come in peace," he said. "I believe you."

They sat there for a while, Niamh nursing her grievances.

Jake said, "The thing about uni, the bit I can't stand, is the people. Walking around like they own the place. Sitting all day on the funds from the trust that Grandpa left them. Knowing that if they need to spend six months on unpaid internship that's fine, the Bank of Mum and Dad will be paying. The ones whose parents bought them a house, so they could let it to their friends, and keep on studying while they kept the other students' rent."

It was an old conversation. He'd had it with Liam, often enough. Niamh's part was to agree with the boys. To indulge them as they played at being proletarians. Which she did, but not without feeling a certain ambiguity in her answers. She looked around the other students and had the vague sense of women clutching Chanel bags, of men whose time stretched out without fear of either jobs or debt. But her boys weren't heroes.

He said, "And they ask you, *Will you come for a drink*? Like it's the biggest deal in the world but they're not going to risk more than one bloody pint, because that one pint is their limit, but you're supposed to sit there, and think you're honoured because it's one beer, and, in their heads, even one beer is this enormous deal, it's such a shock to the system that they're going to write to their parents, and say, I had a beer, Mum. You'd be so proud of me. I did a wee in the toilet, and I flushed. A whole beer, all by myself." Jake took a deep breath, "Jesus, I miss Liam. You could talk to him about this stuff."

"You can talk to me."

"I will. Let's do that." He smiled, before continuing, "There's something else. I was wrong, and I apologise–"

"For what?"

"For ignoring you after Liam died. I'm sorry for sitting in my room and losing myself in my own grief so that for weeks I didn't call–" There was guilt in his eyes, and sorrow, and something else, too – a gleam, as if he was enjoying this act of self-abasement.

"Go on," said Niamh.

"And if I gave the impression that in the Great War of Liam's friends I was siding with Aitch, I'm sorry for that as well. I didn't mean to–"

"I thought, the two of you. You know–" *were making the two-backed beast.*

He looked away. "I want to be clear, and let you know that I won't make the same mistakes again. I can be like a kid sometimes, I hate it when I bear a grudge. I'm not proud. I was out of order, I get it. I do and, from here on in, I will be a much better friend to you." At that, he smiled. He looked at her. His look said, *Your turn.*

But Niamh didn't want a turn. She listened to the murmur of the trees, struggling away in the sky above her. At last, and with some reluctance, Niamh said, "I don't care who's right or wrong. What I care about is this – she's taken Liam away from me. She's got everyone pretending that she knew Liam, she loved Liam, and no one else did. Well, what about me? Don't I have a right to miss him, can't I mourn him too?"

"You do, you should."

She said, "I accept your apology, but why now? It's been weeks. You could have spoken to me anytime."

"I wanted to." Jake said, "I did. I'd wake up each morning, and I'd tell myself today was the day, and I'd call. Then, every time I saw you, you've been looking at me like I shot your pet rabbit. I'm not blaming you – but it made it harder."

"So, I'm the culprit?"

"I'm not saying that."

Jake was smiling again, and deeper than before. He spoke. Then, with a twinkle, "Also Liam's mum's been calling, every day. I love her to bits, but it's too much. I couldn't give her your number, could I – would you take one for the team?"

Niamh said, "Deirdre. Her name's Deirdre." Then, not bothering any more to conceal the relief in her voice, she continued, "I've missed you more than anything."

Niamh went back to Vron's maisonette. She pulled out her copy of Malone's History and sat in the chair reading it. According to the author, a mermaid had spoken to the soldiers as they prepared to fight for Arthur. They were near Wigan, on the banks of the River Douglas, a place of green grass, white cliffs and golden sands. It was the evening, geese on spits, larks sprinkled with cinnamon. The Saxons on the far side, with feasts of their own. As the soldiers drank their wine, the mermaid and her kin went among Arthur and his knights. They said that if Arthur's knights followed them, they would show them a secret path. But this was a ruse. For, as the knights set off, the water spirits had sent them into a stream, The water was deeper than Arthur's men had thought possible. The creatures laughed as the mortals struggled. A dozen men drowned in their chainmail suits. The merfolk almost killed Arthur himself – would have secured Morgana's revenge were it not for Sir Gawain who rescued him.

Niamh was thirsty. She went to the kitchen, poured a glass of milk, returned to the room. She dropped it, sending jagged shards of glass skittering over her floor.

For there, in the chair where Niamh had been reading, was a woman. Dark glasses, blue drainpipe jeans, little older than Niamh. A necklace of ebony and ivory blocks. Mirelle Jones.

Niamh said, "How the hell did you get in?"

"Your landlady."

"If she'd asked me, I wouldn't have given my permission."

Niamh paused for some remorse in her visitor's face, got bored of waiting. She bent down to pick up the pieces of glass. The effort tired her. It took such a length of time, that – she hoped – it would make the stranger feel uncomfortable. She looked up and saw Mirelle smile at her with a look of exaggerated innocence.

"Why did you come here?" said Niamh.

"You've been hiding from her."

There was no need to ask who *her* was.

"I needed a rest. That's all it was, a chance to recover," said Niamh, knowing as the words came out how unconvincing they sounded.

"She needs you."

"She doesn't."

"I've tried," the woman answered. "These last few weeks, you don't know what she's been like. She's been a ball of rage. There's nothing I can do to calm her."

"If she didn't go round killing people, maybe she'd have

more friends."

"She's got no shortage of them," said Mirelle.

Niamh grunted, looked for the last shard of glass.

Mirelle said, "There are places you can go which she can't follow. The Sandens, *him*, their home. It's too far for her – you know how it works. She can't leave London without help. She relies on other people."

"I get what Jenny wants. She'll go to the house. She'll find the old man and kill him –but what about his descendants? They can't all be guilty."

"She'll help you. She looks after her people."

"From what?" said Niamh. "I don't have any enemies."

"And you're sure about that? The girl – she plots against you. She says prayers to Jenny in her sleep, would turn her against you."

"I'm willing to believe the best of my friends."

"As Jenny would with you. The two of you made a pact," said Mirelle, her lips beaming, but an edge of fatigue ringing around her eyes.

"I *did*," Niamh countered. "And that's the point, isn't it? I did; we don't have it anymore. Look, Jenny helped me for a time – I felt stronger around her. But did she tell you about Hector? I was *inside him* when he died."

"She asks a great deal of her friends."

"Couldn't she be more normal? She doesn't like men, I get it, but couldn't she scare them a little, push them around – and stop there? She doesn't have to be a fucking psycho."

"It gives none of us any pleasure."

Niamh said, "I won't be an accessory."

"And nor will we."

"You could stop her any time."

Mirelle sat there a while. "This is what she told me once. *I do not dance, I cannot sing. I write in water.* She didn't choose this life. None of us did."

"If she's trying to do some good, she could work for a refuge. She could go to the battered women and build a hostel for them."

"You don't think we've considered it?"

Niamh said, "Who's this *we*?" When Mirelle didn't answer, Niamh continued, "Who helps her, all of London's lost women? Why hasn't anyone ever asked me to join?"

Mirelle laughed. "You're asking that – when you've locked your door against her?"

Niamh said, "Well it's been such a pleasure meeting you. Do pass on my regards to Jenny. Tell her, I hope everything works out in the end." She scowled at Mirelle, waiting for the woman to stand, and leave.

Mirelle sat where she was, smiling. She said, "It's your fault, you know."

"What is?"

"*This*," Mirelle said, her tone rich with scorn. "All of it. She wouldn't even be here if it wasn't for you."

"That again? She's told me that before. She's a creature of vengeance. She knew how furious I was with Liam. My anger summoned her. I was reacting to how he'd hurt me. I get it. I'm the one to blame." Niamh was sharing deep secrets. If Mirelle had been capable of decency, she would have bowed her head, apologised for wasting Niamh's time, but none of that happened. Instead, the woman remained sitting where she was, her little smirk broadening into a grin. "It's the truth," Niamh said. "If you don't like it, you can leave."

"It's not what she told me," the woman replied.

Niamh was staring at her, fighting the urge to strike the woman in her face.

"What Jenny said was this. You'd lost your boy. You wanted him back from the girl who'd taken him. That's why

Jenny came to you – you stank of jealousy."

"Get the hell out," Niamh said.

Later, as she sat on the bus, she was reading *The Book of Margery Kempe*. Her heart hadn't altogether settled from earlier. She was remembering reading it before, staring at the pages as they slipped out of her hand. She'd listened to some music. Not in her own room. She didn't want to be in the same room where that stranger had told such awful lies. She'd sat in the kitchen. She pinched one of Vron's fags and smoked it. She walked around the kitchen, knocked over a plate. She left it where it lay. Niamh smashed her hand into the table, hard enough to break it. She dug her nails into the skin below her thumb, screamed out in fury.

She imagined herself thanking God with all her heart, as Margery Kempe had, for allowing her to complete her pilgrimage to Jerusalem, the City of Heaven. Margery had slipped from her mount, the passers-by rushing to her attention, reviving her with smelling oils, and spices. For days after, the passers-by had gone to her side, served her every need. Women martyrs, women monsters – the two categories were closer than they seemed.

She and Jake had arranged to meet at eight. She made it to the Chapel Bar before seven. She sat in the lounge drinking Guinness in honour of Liam. Niamh imagined the virginal white of the pilgrim's clothes, remembered the fourteen children Margery had left behind in Leicester. Niamh had dressed up before she left. High heels, the reddest lipstick in the bathroom cabinet, a white dress. Her hand was still sore from earlier.

At last Jake came in, wearing the leather jacket he'd been born in. They hugged. "We must stop meeting like this," he said. He told her he'd been spending three evenings a week working in a factory assembling motherboards for laptops. Work did him good. The flesh around his face had subsided. In the winter, he'd drunk so much there'd been a greyish tint to his skin. Tonight, he was as pink as a prawn.

He bought her a drink. At the back of the pub, there was a bar billiards table. He'd never played. She tried to adjust Jake's stance. Niamh made him line up the cue beneath both eyes before he shot, but he wouldn't straighten his back. He hooked the balls right. He was so bad at it that she found herself wondering if he was letting her win. She downed another Guinness. The second of the night. The drinks before he'd arrived didn't count.

They took their pints and sat in the beer garden while Jake finished off his cigarette. He was pressing buttons on his iPhone. "Your mistress writes," Niamh said.

"It's more complicated than that."

"Let's walk," she told him. Having visions of the two of them walking in each other's steps, their hearts hammering out a common beat.

"Yes, let's," he said, but he didn't move.

There was rain in the sky, spits and spots unwelcome to the crowd of people gathered in the beer garden. People stood, shook their heads, made their way inside.

With woozy eyes, Niamh watched the rain fall. She downed her next drink. Then the one after that. She reached in her bag. Keys, cash, Oyster card.

Jake said, "Did you know that alcohol contains this very special hormone, an anti-diuretic, and it stops you passing too much water?" He said, "But there's this point. Six, seven pints in, and the hormone stops working. All anyone can do is pee."

"My dad was a pub landlord." She corrected herself, "Wanted to be a landlord."

Niamh's dad had left one morning and come back at

teatime saying he'd signed on the dotted line for a pub lease. "It's got eight ensuite rooms," he'd said, "And two bars. It's what we've always dreamed of." Except they hadn't. Sure, they'd had big hopes, but different ones. They'd hoped to clear the gutters, so the rain didn't come in through the ceilings. They'd planned to sort out the kitchen tap which was always stuck. They'd imagined going back to Spain in the summer. They'd never thought of owning a pub. He had, it was his Land of Cockaygne, his long-cherished dream, and *he* wasn't *they*, was it?

Jake asked if she knew the one about the man that watered the workers' beer. She didn't. It felt to Niamh as if she was losing control of the evening. If this was going to be the romantic occasion she'd been hoping for, shouldn't he have produced some chocolates by now, some flowers, shouldn't he be asking her back to his room?

Jake sang to her, "I'm the man, the very fat man that waters the workers' beer," and he gave her a look, such a serious look that she couldn't help but giggle.

She shook her head and laughed. As she did, she loosened inside.

"There it goes," Jake said. Lifting the phone to his eyes.

"Goes what?"

Snap, the phone went. Snap-snap-snap.

"What?"

"The workers' beer." He pointed the camera downwards. Snap-snap-snap.

She looked down, saw the bottom half of her dress, the unforgiveable dark line stretching down the insides of her dress. She felt the warmth, the cruel warmth.

"You bastard," she said.

"Serves you right for what you did to Helen," he told her. Jake was still allowed to call her that. He reached down with both hands to the phone. Then lifted it more. Stuck the camera right in her face. A red light came on.

"You toerag, you dick." She jumped at the phone. He grabbed both her wrists. She tried to kick him. Still filming, he twisted her to the side.

"You shit-gibbon," she screamed, over his mocking laughter.

Then, bored of this game, Jake reached out and shoved her. She slipped, became a mess of uncoordinated movement, clattered to the ground.

He said, "Don't ever mess with her again."

The sound of the door closing behind Jake.

The worst thing was the bartender's kindness, "Are you all right? Should I call a taxi. Do you need some water?" No, she told him. No.

It was all too much for Niamh. She curled up on the ground like a toddler.

Before leaving her accommodation the next morning, Niamh gathered in her hands the last of the objects she'd brought from home. She needed to make Jenny an offering – something that was a loss to Niamh. A gift that would prove the reality of her remorse. She chose a pewter tankard, smoothed down as it was by age. Someone had stamped the number 46 on its back, the year of its making, Niamh supposed. The light shone off its surface, from its lid. The Rose, Shipston. She could remember when the mug had come into her life. Her dad had waved the tankard at Niamh's mum, cited it as evidence. Used it to prove that the pub was a worthwhile investment. It had history, you see. The pub had been at the same location for fifty years, for a hundred years. It was the oldest pub in all of Warwickshire. Not that that the tankard had helped his argument. Instead, her mum had gripped her face tight, insisted her dad go on alone. When he left, Niamh had hidden the vessel in her room. She'd thought if she kept the mug safe, secured it from her mother's careful eyes, he'd have to come back.

If not for her or her sister, then for his mug at least.

Clutching the mug in her right hand, Niamh walked down the hill to where the canal appeared. She found Jenny's tunnel, her ledge.

The city retreated into the distance. She waited. A gentle breeze played around her, a light air. She waited until she could feel the waters of the canal lapping against the stone walls that held them, the little stones clinking in the waves.

Niamh felt a presence, the same black dress. Jenny had accessorised it, adding a red flower to her black shawl.

"Was Mirelle not a beacon? Did she not warn thee?"

"She did," Niamh acknowledged, "I should have listened to her, and I didn't."

"Thy peevish pride."

Niamh held out her tankard, saw Jenny take it. She said, "I won't make the same mistake again. I promise."

CHAPTER 11
ESCAPE ARTIST

The next morning, Niamh had told her landlady she was going away for the week. Not a holiday, she'd said. It was research for her dissertation. "You must love those books an awful lot," Vron said, in a voice that could have curdled milk, "if you're travelling for a whole week to be with them." Niamh told her that it was the highlight of the course, getting her hands dirty with research. Tirzah jumped on Vron's French dresser. Stood there, rumbling, demanding attention with the desperate self-pity of a down-at-heel aristo.

"There's a woman, my friend." Niamh had paused at that word, winced as she spoke it. She had invited Jenny back into her life. Jenny was once again as much a part of Niamh's life as pillows and pyjamas. But that was her decision, and she'd made it.

Niamh said, "What I'm asking is have you ever had an ally, and you wanted to help them, but at the same time you weren't sure?"

Vron paused before answering. She said, "I don't think so. You see, at my age, we're past all of that. If you've got a chum who never listens to you, why suffer them?"

"That's it. She does her own thing," sighed Niamh. She wanted to explain it but there were depths to this dilemma, and she couldn't articulate them.

After that, she was leaving London. As she stood beneath the concrete vault of Euston station, she remembered a painting she'd seen, of the same building at the birth of the railway age, the whiskered Victorian gentlemen with their top hats. They held fishing-rods clasped in one hand, dog-leashes in the other. The train was a source of order; it was an alternative to chaos. It was rationality, prosperity, the physical expression of British industrial power.

A century of London life had blown away the steam, lightened the blackened bricks beneath which past generations had huddled. Progress had delivered Italian delicatessens, French patisserie, a mechanical departure board which clattered like an army of monkeys typing out bad verse. The passage of time had increased the cost too, made a form of transport which had been available to the majority into an indulgence which she struggled to justify. And yet, for all of that, a train was still an adventure. It was an escape from the ordinary, and her mood was one of anticipation. She would find the Sanden home and confront Edward, if he still lived, and secure for Jenny the justice she deserved.

She'd booked on the 10:30. The 8:30 was still showing (delayed), as was the 9:05 (delayed), and the 9:30 (delayed). As she looked at the board, the 9:30 changed from delayed to cancelled. The concourse was heaving with passengers.

At last, the train came. Niamh chose a seat near the front of the train. The carriage was quite as busy as you'd expect. Three middle-aged men walked in after her, sat on the table around her, dropped beers clinking in a white Tesco carrier bag at their feet.

Beyond the glass lay the greasy black brickwork of the nineteenth-century rail network then the flat, drab, fields of Buckinghamshire and Staffordshire. The train made its slow, awkward way juddering on the track. Freight carriages stood abandoned at the track side.

It was June and the men were going to watch the cricket. At least they weren't paying any attention to her. The rain thickened, beat upon the glass.

The driver applied the brakes. Slower the train went and slower still. The gloom inched past beyond the window. She wondered if this was one of those districts where the track was at its oldest and needed replacing. With a final, anxious squeak the train came to a complete halt. Niamh's fellow travellers – regulars on this route, she reckoned – did not lift their eyes from their drinks, no one swore. They were used to the delays, in the same way they'd acclimatised to everything else about the new world being born around them, the boarded-up shops on the high street, the NHS waiting lists, the community centre with its new food bank.

The train stopped at Tamworth. "Apologies for the late running of this service. If your train is more than 15 minutes late you may be eligible for compensation."

Niamh closed her eyes, willed herself to sleep.

Niamh had spoken to Jenny. They'd met at the canal side. Niamh had asked her if she liked being in London. "In thy Metropolis they do incline to sadness," she said. "The people sit as still as statues. Others rot alone in mansions large enough to satisfy a king. If I was to walk among them unhidden, would they accept me?" Niamh wanted to say there were good things about the city, the parties, the crowds that gathered at New Year. That was the best of London, the people who tolerated anything. By the time she'd worked out what she meant to tell the water spirit, it was too late. She wasn't sure either answer would have satisfied Jenny's question. Instead, she asked Jenny about Sanden.

How could Jenny be so confident of her war with him? What was the point of going to his house, when according to every record he'd died four hundred years before?

"He lives," Jenny insisted.

"But his burial is listed in the parish registry."

"The boy knew him," said Jenny – she meant Hector.

When Jenny was in a mood to be stubborn, she withdrew. She did not rage, nor would she stamp her feet. Such public displays of anger were beneath her, but nor did she back down. Persuaded of the truth of some fancy, she would cling to it, refuse all other explanation.

"All right, why Edward?" Niamh asked.

"He was at the assize."

"What assize?"

"He was to me cruelty itself," Jenny answered, but no matter how Niamh pressed her, she wouldn't elaborate. She clung to the water, kept her eyes elsewhere.

The most practical information Niamh coaxed out of Jenny was this: she could summon Jenny using the same method as before; London water would do the trick, even at two hundred miles. Speak her name and Jenny would come.

Through the rest of the evening, with the help of caffeine but with precious little enthusiasm from Jenny, Niamh used her phone to find out facts about Sanden Hall. It had survived civil wars, the shift of the population to the cities. When other private houses in the district had ended up in the hands of the National Trust, the Sanden descendants still occupied the Hall, stared out from behind its antique windows. Niamh had found a Victorian photograph of its exterior. In those black and white images, ivy covered its walls like a second skin. It seemed to her a dark and hostile place, but she remembered the images of the house she had seen in Hector's final vision. He'd grown up in that dark mansion, had been happy there.

Jenny had spoken of a trial. Niamh found a database on her phone. There was a summary of the hearing, which she read to her companion. "Meg Waite, a Woman of about 60 years of Age, and five of her confederates, were indicted for Witch-Craft, and using several Diabolic Arts, by which they sought to kill one Anne Sanden, a Girl about 13 years of Age. The Father of the Complainant gave Evidence, that the accused first Bewitched his Daughter, a while after that his Daughter fell into a most piteous Condition, but the said Meg Waite produced evidence that she had lived an honest life, and that she went to Church."

The document ended there.

"What was the verdict?"

Silence.

"All right, tell me about Meg Waite then," Niamh asked.

Jenny scowled.

Niamh's question, "What did Sanden have against you, anyway?" produced no more illuminating answer. She asked, "When did you see him last?"

"His face was ever in my eyes until I woke."

That may well have been true, but it wasn't what Niamh was asking.

Mirelle had been there, too, sitting beside Jenny, tolerating Niamh's questions, the long silence which met them. "Tell her about the others," she said.

"I was not the first," said Jenny, in a bitter voice.

"Go on," said Mirelle.

Turning to face Niamh, Jenny said, "Others lived in the water before me." Niamh swallowed. "When I was a child, the boys fetched hazels and catkins, then fought over them. It would last till dark put a stop to it. They considered the catkins the spoils of war. The sport was to the boys the height of their ambition. They fought to prove their dominion over the pond. They would say to one another – that tree, if they could reach it, if they walked across the green carpet that lay upon the water – they would have found a victory. And, even as they spoke those words, they knew that beneath the surface a peg was waiting. They called her the Greenteeth. Her, with the skinny paws and the sharp teeth and a sore fear she was to all the children. It was a game for the cruel boys and their milksop companions – she fed on the latter."

"It sounds like a fairy tale," said Niamh.

Mirelle was more practical, "If there were others then, could there be more of you now?"

"I would feel their presence."

"It's not impossible, though, is it?"

"I would not wish my present life on my worst enemy."

Niamh didn't like the turn the conversation had taken. "The Jenny in your story, did she eat the boys up?"

"More or less."

"Either she ate them, or she didn't," said Niamh. "It can't be both."

"She did as I do. She swam with them in the water."

"And what about girls?"

"She gave them as many chances as they deserved; she had no reason to treat them with aught but kindness. They respected her."

After the interview had concluded, Mirelle escorted Niamh back to the lights of London. The cars buzzed through the streets ahead of them. Mirelle wheezed as they walked, carrying pain in her body – the physical expression of her frustration with Niamh. Whatever she had done wrong, Niamh didn't want to know.

"Can you I join your club?" she asked Mirelle at last.

"What club?" Mirelle answered, furrowing her brow.

"Your great society, the survivors of male violence."

"Who said there was any such thing?"

"You did, when you came to my house." Niamh sighed. "I'm sorry, I know I can be a bit much sometimes, I get angry when I don't mean to. But I'm being serious, if there's a group of you and you're helping Jenny, then good on you. If you have meetings–"

"We don't."

"Well, whatever it is, if there's anything I can do, ask."

"I asked you to help," Mirelle Jones said, "and you agreed. That's plenty."

Niamh stared at her, tried to work out whether to believe her. But Mirelle had her eyes on the pavement, wouldn't look at her.

Niamh must have been more tired than she realised. By the time she woke, they were arriving at Manchester Piccadilly. She checked her watch – four hours since she'd left London. The train, which had begun late, and become later still, was passing into a fresh territory of such an exuberant delay its arrival would become a cause for celebration.

She changed onto the stopper service. She sat down beside a middle-aged woman in a navy-blue smock, a wooden cross badged to her chest. The second train was old, the stitching of the seats faded. The windows were caked with dirt. Niamh told herself to sleep this part of the journey away. At Clifton she woke for a moment, sat up, thought of resting once more.

"There you are," the woman said. "I don't mean to pry. I hope you don't mind, but I saw your book. I remember reading it years ago – I loved it."

"This old thing–" Niamh looked down. *The Death of Cats*, she'd borrowed it from the university library. In the chapter which gave the book its name, a young man travelled to Georgian London. He was apprentice to a printer, where he lived a life of ease. The one sadness was his employer's two dozen cats. They howled for food, refused to sleep, kept the apprentice up all night. He persuaded his master that a demon occupied their bodies. The printer ordered the boy to drown them. Then, back from that act of mass felicide, the story pulled. Cats were witches' familiars, the author noted. They were a symbol of cuckolding – the apprentice was taking a solicitous interest in his master's wife. Killing kittens, the historian wrote, was easier than killing bosses. "I like it too," said Niamh, "but it's rather gruesome."

"Isn't it?" The woman grinned her approval. "As, I'm afraid, is today's weather," she continued, turning her eyes to the window, and the downpour outside.

"Niamh."

"Isidore – or Sister, if you'd rather."

"If it's like this in Chorley–"

"Which it will be," the woman answered. "If not worse."

"Then I'll be glad of the two sweaters I packed."

"It's the Fells," Sister Isidore said. "Even in summer–"

Niamh lifted her eyes to the glass, where the rain was landing, making armies of the drops which landed, blew off, and generated replacements. There hadn't been many nuns in Niamh's life, and she was in awe of the stranger.

The train stopped at a little country station. "Apologies for the late running of this service. If your train is more than 15 minutes late you may be eligible for compensation."

They were deep in the north Lancashire countryside. This was a quite different world from where the train had started. The ground rose and fell in sudden hills. Fields stood fallow; the weeds grew wild. Birch and elm explored the sky. Then their route took the train once more back to terraced houses, disused factories, warehouses – the decaying beside the new. On the vehicle went, making the same unsteady progress as before.

Sister Isidore asked, "What brings you up here, anyway?"

"History."

"Go on."

"Sanden Hall," said Niamh, "the poet who lived there, his relative the soldier. I love the way they're all stuck together, so close in time, and within a few years–"

"We'd chopped the King's head off?"

"That's it," said Niamh though how she'd been planning to finish the sentence was with one of the euphemisms people had used to escape the fact that two hundred thousand people had died. The Great Rebellion, it somehow sounded less threatening.

"He deserved everything he had coming to him," the woman said.

Niamh smiled. "I thought you'd be for the other side?"

"The Kings? Because of how I'm dressed?"

"Something like that."

Isidore laughed. She said, "Niamh, with a name like that, I'm guessing you were brought up Catholic?"

"Kind of. On my mother's side." Although her mum had stopped going to church not long after Niamh was born.

"I'm sure a well-read young woman like you has heard of the Second Vatican Council? Or of liberation theology? You must know that millions of Catholics, the world over, are committed to social justice." Sister Isidore peered at Niamh, then stopped herself. She seemed to shrink in her seat. "Sorry, I don't mean to make speeches."

"No, do go on."

The old woman had shown so much passion, but the gulf between the generations had stretched too wide. For the first time, a silence fell between them.

Niamh felt she'd disappointed her companion. She said, "I had a look on the map, and there isn't a footpath, let alone a road. Was it built like that?"

"There's a private road. Make it to the reservoir, and you

can walk up from there. Well, in theory you can – the Sandens aren't too keen on visitors."

Niamh said, "You've seen them, yourself?"

"They are the talk of the village."

"It sounds like something out of Hansel and Gretel."

"Oh no, much worse than that," Sister Isidore laughed.

"Were you a teacher? Before, I mean–" It was the way, she could deliver a reprimand in a look then defuse the tension with a smile.

"For a while, evening classes," Isidore said. "But that was a whole lifetime ago."

Niamh waited for an elaboration but there was none. "I'm looking forward to exploring," she said, with more bravado than she felt.

The nun peered at the tankard sitting beside Niamh's right hand. She said, "If you don't mind me asking, what's that?"

"This mug?"

Isidore said, "The way you're clutching it, I supposed it must be valuable."

Niamh looked down, saw that her hand was indeed gripping Jenny's tankard. She let go. "Sentimental value," she said. "It was my dad's."

"Honour your father and mother," Isidore recited, "so that it may go well with you, and you may enjoy a long life on this earth."

Niamh sat there, wondering if she was supposed to say, *Amen*. With an effort she said, "The Sermon on the Mount?"

"The Ten Commandments. We'll be at Chorley in less than an hour," Sister Isidore told her. "If you'd like to save yourself the cost of a taxi, I'd be happy to give you a lift."

Isidore drove an ordinary little car, a copper Volkswagen Golf. It had seen better days. There was a rosary hanging down from the rear-view mirror. "Wool country," she said, as the car started, and there were indeed any number of adolescent lambs, their mothers ignoring them, concentrating on their food. Niamh twisted the tankard as if to give Jenny a view, counted down the seconds until the two of them would be alone.

Isidore drove Niamh to the pub where she was staying. Her face darkened, "You're not planning to be here tomorrow in the day, are you?"

"No. I'll be going over to Sanden Hall."

The nun shook her head, as if somehow dissatisfied with Niamh's answer. She reached to her lapel, onto which a little wooden cross was pinned. Opening it, she attached it to Niamh's sea-green blouse. "Humour me," she said. "It will protect you."

Niamh started to protest. "I shouldn't. I'm not–" She started to say *a believer* but faced with the fact of Isidore's calling the word seemed disrespectful.

"It will give me some comfort, to think you aren't on your own." Isidore smiled, "I'm here with my daughter – I lived a full life before I chose the church. She lives in Thinch, it's two miles west of here," she took out a piece of paper and wrote down an address and a phone number. "Any time you need a change of scenery, do call."

"I will," Niamh promised.

Her destination was a gastro pub with its menus pinned to the walls, the dishes ranging from the small-but-dear to the just-past-expensive. Niamh sat at the dark wooden table, beside a plain white wooden wall. She had the place to herself. She ordered a dandelion and burdock. The inn was quieter than she'd expected. She remembered the many rural pubs she'd visited with her father, how he'd coaxed stranger into telling him their life stories. The inn would have seemed hostile to him, she reckoned – fussy, empty. Not the busy meeting place that he'd loved. No fires, no stories, no local knowledge. She waited in vain for the sounds of contented drinking breaking up around her, for the warning to keep clear of the full moon.

She went upstairs. Niamh's room was on the first floor, with little trinkets in it to make the guests feel that the expense was merited: a porcelain stag, a wooden globe. Through the window, she could see a country road, a red phone box, a crossroads of sorts. That's where you met the devil, didn't you, at the meeting of roads?

She put out the tankard holding Jenny's water.

On one wall, a series of pencilled rings had been drawn in the plaster. There were nine of them, and in the middle a dot, ringed black, "Sol," the sun. The first ring, Mercury, the second Venus. Around the third a dot turned – "Terra," the earth. She'd seen the image before, Copernicus's drawings of the celestial orbs. She wondered how long it had been there, Reason, keeping her perfect watch over the ignorant folk.

Facing it, hung a print – a portrait of King James I. It was small, little larger than a book cover, and yet it dominated the wall. Niamh approached the painting. She recognised its subject from the textbooks on her History course – his grey beard, his constant scowl of disappointment. There'd been so many things to dissatisfy him: the stroke he'd suffered, the gout, the dysentery, his kidney stones. He'd sworn down God's vengeance on his ailments. On abandoning his Scottish kingdom, he'd been little happier with the habits of his English subjects, their lust for tobacco, their gluttony and superstition. The artist had painted King James in a silver jerkin and jaunty trousers, but the effect was jarring. His clothes warred with his grim expression. The monarch stood beside a forest. The horse beside him bowed, marking nature's obedience to its Sovereign, while the wind blew James's hair out of place, discomforted the monarch who glared at the horse, at the rainclouds. She could imagine him leading a troop of his soldiers against the Deity who had chosen this day to rain.

"You were a misery-guts weren't you?" she told the painting.

The landlord knocked on the door, to check that the room was to her satisfaction. He was younger than she'd expected. Shy. He said, "Will you be about tomorrow – in the day?"

"I'll be out, exploring."

He nodded, "Good on you, lass."

It wasn't until after he'd gone that she remembered that Isidore had asked the same question. In both cases, they'd been grateful of Niamh's plans to be away from the inn. Well, so what, if she was missing something? She needed to find Sanden Hall – that was her mission.

Niamh watched the tankard, thought of summoning Jenny. "Not today," she said. "I'll wait till I've got some proper news."

After that, the rest of the evening was quiet. The rain had stopped; the wind too had died down to nothing. From downstairs came the hum of many voices, all jumbled up together. Niamh left the curtains undrawn, switched the light off.

Hers was a deep, contented, sleep.

CHAPTER 12
AN INDEX OF WATER

When Niamh woke, the air was cold, as if the weather had gone back a month at least – from June in London to May or April in Chorley. The covers were warm, and she was in no hurry to leave them. She could hear the morning chorus of thrushes gossiping outside her window. She felt better rested, happier than she had in weeks. Niamh breakfasted, ate an egg and cheese on a thick Lancashire cob. She walked out from the pub into the countryside. Her thoughts whirred round and round. She formed stratagems to talk her way into the Sanden home, discarded them. A dew-covered footpath led through working fields towards the woods. The hills kept her mood light. She was determined to enjoy the morning.

The Birmingham in which she had grown up was a flat country from which all trees had been excised, a place of red-brick municipal buildings and Methodist halls. Her parents fought the urban by hiking. In summer, they took her and Yvonne away by train and taught them the names of wild things. As she explored the hills around Sanden Hall, she recognised the glints of purple, their heads bowed at the approach of a stranger. They were Bitter Vetch. Those yellow gems, Hay Rattle; the white globes Cat's Ear. That sweet, fetid, tang on the air was Wild Garlic. The birds tormenting each other were plovers and curlews.

Onwards the fields went, sloping down towards woods and water. This district had never been busy, but there had been many more people living here four hundred years ago.

She descended. As she walked through the trees, the sun drifted behind clouds. The wind rose again, twisted the rowan trees, caused the birches to shiver.

She came at last to the place where Jenny's home had stood. Niamh had found a map online - Grace Foster, the village apothecary, owned a cottage in these very fields. As had her neighbour Elizabeth Dickenson, midwife. Jenny – then called Jennifer Gill – lived here too.

The fields around this place had once been marshland with a narrow river running through the middle. After the war, one of the nearby town councils had voted to flood the low ground. Among the buildings lost to the water was the house in which Jenny had lived. The inrushing liquid had swept away the two-storey home, two up, two down, scattered the stained glass from the windows. An inlet ran down the side of the hill from above.

As for Jenny's house itself, there was nothing, no lath, no plaster, not an indentation in the ground to mark where the building had stood.

Niamh said, "You didn't live anything behind, did you?"

Into the ink-black depths of the water, she peered. She saw tree-roots which had grown together in the darkness. A dark, dank place, shapes that came and went.

She looked up and, for the first time, saw Sanden Hall. Niamh had studied the district on maps. She knew that there were three joined expanses of water. She hadn't realised that it was possible to see from here all the way to the brick monstrosity at the lake's far end – its windows a bastille, the citadel sneering down on these bucolic ruins.

Seeing her destination, Niamh shivered. Already she was planning, looking to each side of the water for a path – there had to be a way, but she couldn't see it. She thought of following alongside the lake but could see nothing more than thick forest, impassable with the trees packed tight against each other. If there was a path – which there had to be – it was on the wood's far side. She hurried away from the lake. On, she went, leaving the waters behind.

She saw the sun squeeze its way through the tops of the verge along which she passed. A stone wall bounded its left edge, bushes its right. Niamh crossed an expanse of empty ground. There were pines in the distance. Her mood lifted, as she walked beside wood anemone and primroses. Keeping the water out of sight, she found herself in an embrace of sunlight.

All the time, Niamh was looking for the route that would lead her to Sanden Hall. She was standing, she reckoned, half a mile beyond the hall. Due west. The path must be close. If she could somehow fly there– She broke off a hazel branch, struck at the weeds at the side of the road, looked for something, anything, to mark the next part of her passage. The way was here; she knew it. She reached into her bag, pulled out her phone, studied her map. The way was here, it had to be, and yet the path ended in a wall of trees. She called on the wood to reveal its secrets. She begged to Jenny for help – without answer.

Niamh was back at the pub by ten, chastened. She ducked her head at the doorway, hoping to avoid the landlord. Her first thought was of going to her room, summoning Jenny. She was tired after the walk. She was annoyed with herself for her failure to find Sanden Hall. And yet, despite everything, it was good to be back. The sun was bright overhead. A hundred people had assembled on the grass verge facing the hotel. Beyond them, beyond the red phone booth, stood a barn. She hadn't noticed the building before, had assumed it was some mere outhouse. None of her business. And yet– Outside the barn, people smiled, embraced late arrivals. They had the eager look of folk awaiting some shared entertainment. Children ran through the crowd, happy as wedding guests,. She could see no white dress, no groom with a rose in his buttonhole, but if Niamh waited long enough, no doubt they'd come. The adults filed into the barn.

"Come on," a man told her. He was in his thirties, velvet jacket. "Everyone in."

For a moment, Niamh was ready to tell him that no, she wasn't part of the crowd. But she felt self-conscious. It was easier to go along with him, with all the others. When she saw the insides of the barn, Niamh was glad she had. The chamber was on two levels. Wooden beams held up the roof; lights hung down, candles in wooden baskets. There was a high oak table, a raised wing to the side. She could imagine some rural fellowship gathering here. It was cool inside; it would have been a good place to mark the gathering of the harvest.

On one wall, hung the same painting of King James that Niamh had seen in her room. This, she guessed, was the original – life-sized. The same jerkin, the ridiculous red trousers.

Niamh felt a presence at her side. Without looking round to see who it was, Niamh addressed her unseen companion, "What a laugh he must have been."

"Pardon, mistress," a voice answered. Masculine, hostile.

Turning to face the man, Niamh felt the ground quiver. His face was thin and large – stretched so long it sagged down and swallowed his neck. She might have said his face was disfigured, but that wasn't the half of it. He was vile to look at, old, beyond hideous. She wondered if some disease could make you look like that. Names came to her from books – syphilis, smallpox, leprosy – but it wasn't any of them, it wasn't even age, it was resentment. His nose and lips had been trapped in a scowl, a look of spite, hatred, and disdain. He had much the same look of scorn on his face as the portrait they were both admiring. But King James was a mere amateur at that art, while this man was the expert. Scars had formed beneath his cheeks. Cancers had grown there, admitted defeat, shrunk back down again to nothing. The skin had withered into his wrinkled face. As it had fallen inwards, it had exposed his cheekbones, his nose, his jaw, making them large, alien. Thick liver-spots bunched together. All his face was white and yellow, corpse-like, but his cheeks were an obscene red. On the pale bulb of his giant head a single strand of grey hair fought on alone.

The feeling of his eyes upon her face was sickening, a horror – as if an insect was crawling upon her skin, down her cheeks, along her jaw.

She realised she was staring. "I'm sorry," Niamh said. "It was a joke. I didn't mean anything." The stranger wore a dark cotton jacket. A jet ribbon stretched around the white collar of his throat. Niamh forced herself to look away. Again, she said, "I'm sorry."

"The painting before you is the likeness of our Sovereign. This village holds a few treasures, and this is the greatest of them."

His face was so close to hers. She thought, for a moment, that he was going to reach out and kiss her. His face contorted. He stared at the wooden cross, pinned as it still was to her blouse. He took a step backwards, cast her another suspicious look.

Niamh wanted to say, *Who painted it?* But she knew how the words would have broken under the man's hostility. It would have seemed like a challenge, and she could no more fight him than could she duel the moon. Her mind was blank, and yet she felt a duty to speak. "What's all this?" she asked, holding out a hand to take in the people, their seats, the table.

"The chase. Before the assize begins."

Then, with a last regretful shake of his antique head, away he strode with steps that were long, slow, and shambling.

The voices in the barn grew louder. Men shook hands, women too, then separated themselves, the men sat on the lower level, while the women found chairs, sat, and watched the proceedings from the raised gallery. The children were still holding back outside the barn. No, one of them had made snuck in. A boy had stolen inside the room, but he wasn't wanted there. The others stood back from him, formed a large, disapproving circle. The boy reached for his father, but his parent gave him a sharp word or two, pointed him back outside. The child ran out, returning to the forgiving sunshine.

Seeing the boy run like that, Niamh wished she could have left with him, but she was on a mission. The Sandens couldn't be far away.

"Better get started," a voice said, louder than the others around it.

A man, jovial-looking and round-faced, strode to the presiding table. Niamh recognised him, the pub landlord. He had dressed up for the occasion and was now wearing a wax Barbour jacket and happy-as-mustard trousers.

"Here we go," the landlord said, lifting a handkerchief in his right hand, leaving it above his head, as a way of motioning for silence. He said, "Now that we've picked our twelve good men and true, we come to the main part of today's ceremony. As I look around the room, I see a few unfamiliar faces an' you're all welcome. It's been a while since we've had one of these, an' if you don't know what to do, that's fine, stick to the back and copy everybody else."

"The hag–" he said.

For a moment Niamh wasn't sure if she'd heard him right.

She stiffened, she wanted to shout out, *Don't you know what century this is? No one uses words like that anymore*. But, as she looked around the barn, there were no scowling faces, no hints of disapproval. Niamh swallowed her protest, made herself attentive again.

"The hag'll set off at eleven," the landlord continued. "The rest of us will follow, a minute after. She'll go left down North Lane, then Tumble Road, Sowberry Street. After that, she can go where'er she wants. An' we'll be looking for her. Find a pace what suits you. We follow, that's all. Kids with their parents, cameras left behind, all pets on leads." He smiled. "Any questions?" He waited, "There were none. Minute that."

He signalled to a woman at his side, "You ready, my love?"

"Reckon I am," the woman said – to a flutter of applause. The hag, Niamh thought, although she hated the word.

"Good on you," the landlord said. "Then it's back here for speeches. Refreshments at one. They're on the house, same as ever."

The people clapped the promise of free food.

Out they went, Niamh following the crowd. The woman from the barn was there, standing at the front in a pool of sunshine. "Five minutes," the landlord shouted, keeping a respectful distance behind her. Niamh had imagined it was going to be a race. Out they'd run, the children in front. The hag, *the woman*, would lead them home.

She studied the woman who was at the centre of their attention. She was old, in her forties at least, but she looked athletic with her long hair tied back. She was wearing an old-fashioned white cotton shirt and beneath it black jogging shorts. Someone had given her a deerskin rug, which she held over her shoulders, left hoof in left hand, right hoof in right. Niamh refused to think of the woman as a hag. *A doe*, that's what she was. Niamh liked that word, considered the woman a thing of nature. She longed for the woman's victory.

The landlord said, "Where's Sanden to?"

Niamh's pulse quickened. *Him*, the old man she'd spoken to. He must be another descendant of Edward Sanden. He'd come down from the big house to glare at the people.

She shuffled back from the crowd, turned round. Within the barn, the landlord was exchanging words with the old man. The latter was complaining, shaking his head in fury. The landlord touched his own chest, bowed his head to his master.

Sanden motioned towards the crowd, pointed at Niamh. She couldn't hear what he was saying, but could tell the gist of it – who had brought that meddling foreigner to this, their private happening? Niamh took a step back, retreating into the safety of the crowd. She didn't think they could do anything to stop her; she hadn't broken any law.

The landlord gave a reluctant smile, rejoined the others.

Sanden leered at Niamh, waved in a sarcastic greeting.

On the dot of eleven the landlord blew a whistle. Off the doe loped – the people cheering as she did. The road had thick bushes on either side. After fifty metres, the path turned. The woman disappeared round the corner. Boys occupied the line behind which the doe had been crouching. Down they went, like athletes before a relay race. The other children stood back from the finish line, stuck their tongues at the show-offs.

The woman at Niamh's side was waving her finger and motioning towards one of the boys in the front. "No phones," she insisted. The boy rushed over, delivered up his device.

The landlord lifted his whistle to his lips, blew.

The boys sprinted at the sound. Within a few metres, they slowed, as if their race had always been to the first corner and no further. Out the sticks came. The rest of the crowd followed. Along the lane they walked, poking with their sticks, bashing wood against branches, hollering, “Come out! Wherever you are.”

Calling this a chase was misleading, Niamh thought, it made you think of races. When the point wasn’t to be fast but thorough. “On!” one of the front-markers shouted, and the crowd quickened. Together, the crowd turned the corner. Onwards the chase went, the children inquiring their sticks into bushes, shouting out as birds fled crying into the sky.

Niamh felt herself entering a dream-state. This was a world of sticks and straw; it was like being inside an antique. She was not in full control of her weight. It seemed to her as if she was no longer in Britain in the new millennium but welcomed back into the past, was living there, was imprisoned there.

The clatter of sticks upon wood. A voice shouting, “Aye, aye, aye.”

Another of the boys cried out, “I’ve seen her! I have! I have!”

“Where?” Faces lifted in excitement.

“An’ you’re sure?”

The boys poked their sticks into the undergrowth.

“No,” they said, their voices desultory.

“You imagined it?”

“I saw her,” the boy said.

“Always one,” his comrade remarked.

One of the younger girls ran for the wildness beyond the hedges. Her mother rushed after her, pointed her back to the procession.

Four times they turned, left, then right; right, then left. The birds cawed above them. On the road led, in a great loop, the sun beating down on them.

"Onwards!" a man cried.

"Keep on," the landlord echoed, from the back of the crowd. He touched a handkerchief to his sweating face.

Another voice cried, "*I see her*."

Then, out of the tall grass where she'd been hiding, the doe strode, deerskin still in place, smoke billowing from her arms. Through the fumes, the children raced. They waved their sticks at the woman, the youngest threw theirs. The teenagers came closer.

The smoke blew away to nothing.

A young woman, tall, slender, was the first to connect. Her bamboo cane swished and hit. Others too. Their attacks broke on the woman's arms. On her body.

Niamh felt sick. It was the way the woman held herself, still, and uncomplaining, not flinching as the blows landed.

A stick struck her full on the face.

Then for the first time, the woman stirred. "Go!" she cried, another blow snapping on her arm. "By all that's wild, I command thee–"

Down the blows fell. Clattering like August rain. She whimpered. A nick on her arm blossomed into a red flower.

The woman took half a step forward to right herself. Her gaze went down.

More blows.

The woman flinched for the first time.

In a whisper, the landlord asked. "Who, hag?" He could have been a teacher in the wings of a school play, reminding one of his charges of their forgotten lines.

An older boy came forward. As he did, the others stood, their heads bowed. They knew his part, respected it. Around Niamh, the crowd settled down into silence.

The boy said, "Who, hag? What power do you command?"

"I command no one."

The boy's stick struck her cheek. She whimpered. He hit the far side of her face. Blood dribbled down, found the gap in the deerskin, turned her white shirt red.

He struck again. Again. The stick splintered. Its last shards fell to the ground. The woman made a little sob, succeeded in stifling it.

Niamh was a raft abandoned at sea. Her guts burned. Her throat thickened with some vile blackness. She, too, was trying to hide her feelings from this crowd of strangers. She knew she should run to the woman's defence but couldn't. To do so would expose her, threaten her mission. And yet, to say nothing in the face of the violence – her inaction made her complicit. She closed her eyes, tried her hardest to will the situation away.

"To the assize," the landlord shouted. One of the girls, it could have been the woman's daughter, so protective she was, took the woman – the doe – by her hand, pulled her back to the road. Away from the danger.

Drunk with the effort of standing, the woman followed.

Another turn, and they were back where they began. At the pub, at the courthouse. The girl found a flannel, cleaned the woman's face. She led her into the barn. There, Sanden was waiting, his arms aloft, a look of delight on his face. After that, it was the same as before, the children outside, the men in the main body of the room, the women seated in respectful silence beside them. Niamh looked around, saw no choice but to sit with the other women.

Sanden waited for the room to settle down into silence. Then he began, "Upon the Command of the Lords of his Majesty's most honourable Privy Council, we have come to this place to hear the testimony against the women charged with this offence. They are in number six, of whom five fall into my knowledge, therefore I can give you my description of them. The first is called Margaret Waite, a widow that some years ago came to dwell in these parts, with her husband. She and her husband brought with them an evil report for witchcraft. The next is her daughter. The third is Jennifer Gill–"

Niamh startled. She'd heard the names before. They were the witches against whom another Sanden had given his testimony, four hundred years earlier. He'd mentioned Jenny too – she'd been another defendant.

The old man said, "Of the victims, two are mine own daughters, and this was their condition when the witches had worked their evil upon them."

On he went, telling the same story that had been told at the trial centuries before. Of witches and their familiars. Of the wax likenesses they made of their victims. Of people who could change shape. "Wickedly, and maliciously," he said, "they did practise their foul acts."

The women around her were like the students on Niamh's course. They offered their teacher their seeming attention, while between them little whispers travelled. "That was a good clout you gave her," one of Niamh's neighbours said.

"An' you too," said the girl beside her, smiling.

The old man was telling the story of the visit to his home, and the wretch, the poor-seeming woman, who had asked his daughter Anne to grind corn for her to make bread. In return, she offered to pay for their service with a penny-piece which she had been wearing on a string around her neck. They might buy with it whatever they pleased. His daughter took the money, saw that the coin had been defaced, refused to accept it in payment. Accepted it against her judgment. The king's visage bent out of shape. From that day on, demons had assailed his children. A deformed thing came with many feet, black in colour, the old man said.

On his words came, low, and yet insistent, "And the creature tortured my child, afflicted, consumed, pined, wasted, and tormented her, by sundry other acts of witchcraft against the peace. For several hours, my daughter did lie for dead–"

Niamh listened to what the old man was saying, found herself imagining his daughter. Alone in the house. Terrified. The illness had been real, she thought – he hadn't invented it.

She felt sick.

She slipped away, out through the barn doors. Niamh gave a desperate look around as she closed them. She needed the comfort of daylight. She felt sick to think of what she'd seen, the smiles on the faces of the children, the woman's passive cries. She would have gone as far as her feet would take her, back to London.

She ran out of the barn, straight into Sister Isidore. "No way–"

"Niamh?"

The two of them looked at one another, in mutual astonishment.

"What are you doing here?"

"I was going to ask you the same question."

Before Niamh could say anything – ask, demand, or explain – she found herself grabbed and hugged. Smothered in more-than-welcome affection.

"What is this?" Niamh asked her.

"I'm sorry – I should have wanted you – I didn't think you'd come."

"What are they doing? Why?"

Isidore said, "I suppose it helps them to make sense of what happened."

"You should have warned me."

"Forgive me," Isidore said. "I have been weak. I thought, I hoped – It isn't the easiest thing to explain." She looked old, tired, and Niamh couldn't be angry with her for long.

"It's the village, this place. When I leave, I find myself forgetting what it's like to live here."

"I'm from Birmingham, the pubs get a bit rowdy, but what the hell was that?"

"I didn't always live here," Isidore looked around. "Until my daughter married–" Her words stopped; her face clouded with unhappiness. The old man must have finished his speech, because the people were coming out, the children rushing towards a table which held food. The nun grimaced, said, "Behind every wall, there are people listening."

Niamh nodded.

The children heaped their shares onto plates.

In a quiet voice, Niamh asked Isidore, "Who's the man?"

"What man?"

Niamh said, "In the barn, he was speaking a moment ago. He looked like those pictures you see in galleries, from years ago. And his skin–"

"Teddy Sanden," whispered Isidore, looking around them, taking a step back to keep her distance from the other participants.

"Teddy?" Niamh said, "I can't believe anyone christened him Teddy."

The landlord clinked a spoon against a glass for silence. He gave a welcoming speech, told them the wine was from Chile, thanked the many villagers who had cooked or laid out their feast. "A good day out," he told them.

Sanden had left the barn, had gone out into the outside air to share in the occasion. The landlord was by his side. He glared past Niamh, grimaced at Sister Isidore.

"You – here?" Sanden said. "With all the accoutrements of your false religion?"

"And you, Edward, risking daylight are you?"

For a moment, the crowd hushed. A hundred pairs of eyes

watched the two antagonists staring at one another, circling like two tom cats, the rulers of their respective kingdoms. Until, at last, the pub landlord forced himself between them, led Sanden away, promising him the chance to meet some important person.

Isidore, too, made her departure.

Food was eaten, jokes exchanged. You would have thought the occasion the most normal of village gatherings, a cricket match. Niamh thought of leaving, wanted to go, but curiosity kept her in the crowd. Then, soon enough, they were heading back.

"You joined us?" The landlord said. "I thought you were goin' out?"

"I did," said Niamh, looking all around her for any sign of her friend the nun. "I tried to." She didn't mention Sanden Hall. She told the first lie that came into her head. "I tried to go to Chorley, but the bus wasn't running." She felt the heat of her cheeks.

"You are a welcome guest," the man said. "Let me get that." Before she could stop him, he reached out. He lifted the cross from her blouse and kept it. "You don't want your good clobber defiled by our country superstitions."

Niamh tried to protest, "But – that's mine."

He was gone before she could stop him.

As Niamh rejoined the company, the same man was standing once more behind the table at the head of the room. As she sat down, he called out, "Let the examination begin."

From the side gallery, away from the company of the other women, a woman walked forward. It was the doe from earlier. She found a seat at some distance from the table, in the full view of the hostile crowd. She kept her eyes cast down, as if ashamed.

In a gentle voice, as if talking to a friend, the landlord asked, "What say you, Margaret Waite, are you guilty of witchcraft?"

At the name Margaret Waite, Niamh felt herself relax. It was a strange response, and not one that was altogether gratifying, but at least she knew what was happening. They were acting out the trial. A local resident must have found a version of the original transcript. This script preserved the very words that others had spoken in this courtroom four centuries before. Knowing that made everything easier somehow. She could breathe.

"I say before God, before whom I stand, that I am no witch."

From those listening came a disbelieving noise, a bitter chuckle.

"Did you hurt Anne Sanden?"

"I did not."

"Did you use magic against her?"

"No, sir, I did nothing of the sort."

"Did you give her name of the Deceiver, carved into a penny piece?"

"I paid for food with the money in my pocket."

"And the coin was defaced?"

"It was not."

The answer did not please the crowd any better than her earlier ones. They itched in their seats, muttered hostile words. "Hag." "Liar."

"Did the witness bring the defaced coin?"

The question was for the witness, but it was the accused – Margaret Waite – who answered, "I tell you, Sir, I did not touch it." She said, "If I would confess to this crime, I would be confessing what is false."

Niamh looked around the room. They must have practised

many times, giving every villager a part to play. Or the words came to them from the past itself. From some shared collective memory, passed down through the generations.

There were more questions, interruptions too. Several times, Margaret Waite had to stop her evidence because, on making her denial, her accusers rose from their chairs and insisted that she lied, spoke to contradict her. One of the young women from earlier came forward. She strode to the front, looking very pretty with her hair bouncing up and down, looking for all the world like she'd prepared it in curling forks. She swore on the Bible.

The girl said that upon the first of October last, she had been taken with a great pain in her stomach. It had felt like someone was stabbing. She told the room that she lay upon her bed, her fists clenched with pain and, when she opened them, her hands were full of little crooked pins, and she could not say who had left them there.

"An' what's to do wi' me?" asked Margaret Waite.

The landlord hushed her.

The young woman said, "You knew, Meg. I told you about it, and you knew already."

"I knew nothing of the sort."

Then away the girl sashayed, back into the crowd.

"How long have you been a witch?" the landlord asked Margaret Waite.

"By the love of God, ah'm not."

It seemed to Niamh that the outcome of this re-enactment of the trial was not the formality that she would have guessed if she'd been asked in advance. At the end of such a hearing, the accused women were convicted, everyone knew that. The system was rigged against them. If they would not confess, they would be ducked in water. If they survived that ordeal, God had rejected them, they could not be innocent.

But the woman playing Margaret's daughter – who came forward as the next witness – was quite as clear in her denials as her mother had been. Asked if she went to church, she answered, "Every week." Asked to repeat the Our Father, she did so with conviction. The cries of protest subsided, the interruptions grew fewer and less confident. In the room, the accused women were having the better of the hearing.

Niamh was surprised, delighted even. Against all her expectations, she found herself enjoying the occasion. She was rooting for the innocent – and they were winning.

From his seat, Edward Sanden growled, "It is all lies, can't you see?"

"No interruptions," the landlord said.

"Can't you see what they're doing?"

"Brother, it is good that you spoke," the landlord said. "We've heard your speech. I can't speak for the other jurors, so these comments are my own. That there are such creatures as witches, I've no doubt; the scriptures say so. The wisdom of all nations has put laws against 'em, but I do say this: if there is any other proof you've got – then bring it. For lettin' the guilty go free, and condemning the innocent, are both an abomination to the Lord."

CHAPTER 13
THE HALL

After the assize had adjourned for the day, which it did soon afterwards without a verdict, Niamh returned to the path which led around the reservoir. She had the benefit on her return of Sister Isidore's detailed instructions as to how to find Sanden Hall. The path kept going, a track between the trees. It passed through oaks and beeches, the wind pressing upon Niamh's face, tearing at her clothes. It would be an exaggeration to call the way a road. No Highways Agency team had ever tarmacked it, but it was wide enough for a car to travel down. The sky darkened. Niamh searched in her bag for her second sweater. The closer she came to her destination, the greater the unease that Niamh felt about the journey. But she remembered the tankard swaddled at the base of her backpack. She couldn't disappoint Jenny.

She reached the point at which the path turned left. She found two abandoned piles of stone and beside them little fallen-down walls. She saw the place where an antique bridlepath, now overgrown, had continued beyond those walls. The footpath bore round to the left. Armed with Isidore's advice, Niamh knew to pause, to look back along the way by which she'd come. Behind her, the road snaked back along the right, obscured by bushes.

At last, she could see Sanden Hall. Niamh remembered the house as she'd seen it on her phone – a tall and spacious building, made elegant by all those windows. In the pictures, it seemed a thing of beauty. It looked different from this approach. Seen from where she was now, the building seemed smaller and less impressive. She was coming upon the house from its side, and, seen from this perspective, the house was shabbier than Niamh had remembered. The windows were few, surrounded by a great expanse of blackened brick. The Hall seemed not the elegant chateau it was from the front, but something meaner, the walls as thick as a prison's. The windows were sealed shut and the curtains drawn against curious eyes. The building was old, tired, with slats missing from several of the shutters, and one of its corners sloping down. The waters of Sanden reservoir lapped within feet of the Hall, forming a natural boundary beyond which no one could pass. So that was how the rich lived, Niamh thought. In miserable isolation from everyone else. She looked on the house and felt pity for its inhabitants.

The plan she'd made was simple in the extreme. Under it, Niamh had one main task. She was going to ingratiate herself with the owners. Inside the Hall, she would find the Sandens. Call Jenny, and the creature would come. Not that they'd ever negotiated what Jenny would do when she arrived, an omission that Niamh was coming to regret. Her friends' appetite for destruction was too strong.

She stood by the doorway. She listened to the songs of the birds, the various parts of the orchestra, some voices chattering away, others low and steady, mere murmurings. She felt the dampness in the air. The water of the reservoir smelled earthy, brackish.

She lifted the heavy knocker; let it fall upon its metal plate.

A woman answered. Brunette, in her fifties at least, the woman's arms escaped the constriction of her pink top. They were scored with eczema, had a texture like fish scales.

"What do you want?" the woman said.

Improvising, Niamh answered. "I hope now's a suitable

time. Please don't think of me as rude, but I'm desperate to ask someone. You see, I'm a History student, and I've read about the Hall, I've been doing my dissertation about it."

She listened to her own words and hated them, thought them pathetic. She said, "I'm fascinated by the Hall, by all the famous people who've lived here. It must be so exciting, isn't it, living in a building like this – like being in a museum?"

Then, emulating the gambler who has bet first a week's salary on red then a month's wages on the same colour, Niamh felt no choice but to continue. Blushing from ear to neck, she said, "I sent a letter asking if I could visit." Another lie but, ignoring it, she continued, "And no one answered. Which left me thinking, they must be busy people. I'm sure they'd have written back if they appreciated how keen I am to look around. If you tell me to go away, I'm not just going to disappear. I'm going to keep on digging."

"I'm sorry," the woman answered. "If you don't mind, student or not. *No visitors*."

Niamh stayed where she was. "Please?"

The woman looked down at the doorway, saw Niamh's shoe wedged in the way. "I'm going to close the door now," she said, "and I'm telling you to remove that toe of yours. Or it won't be my fault if I break it."

Niamh said, "Did you know it was Edward Sanden who built this building? He was a Puritan. They all were round here. They get such bad press but there were good things they did too. Like translating the Bible into English. They banned bear-baiting and cock-fighting – which must have been good for the animals."

"Why, girl, are you still talking?"

"I'm telling you what it says in the books," replied Niamh. She continued, "You know the strangest thing that occurred to me? I thought to myself, what if Edward Sanden's relatives were still alive? What if his descendants were living in the very same house that he'd occupied. I bet they'd have all sorts of interesting stories. The thing I'd like more than anything else, would be to ask them questions. I'd want to know how he dealt with those witches that besieged this house. You must have heard the legends, how the demons captured his daughter's soul. I'd write down everything the Sandens told me."

The woman seemed to sway. But then she righted herself, looked at Niamh with an expression of hatred. "All those words, you're giving me a headache."

"Aspirin's good for that."

"You're not funny."

"Can I come in now?"

To Niamh's disappointment, the woman did not move. She occupied the doorway, a resolute obstacle. "I've told you to go."

"Yes, you have," said Niamh. "And I didn't move. How about this? You speak to Teddy Sanden. See what he says. If he won't speak to me, that's fine, I'll go. But let him choose. I know he's here; I saw him in the village earlier. The whole village saw him."

"If the Sandens say you need to leave, you'll accept their decision?"

"Brownie's honour," said Niamh. She crossed her fingers behind her back, and whispered to herself, *Work me some magic, Jenny.*

Niamh was led into a drawing room, full of antique things. A fireplace dominated one wall. There were two large sofas, busy with cushions. The textiles were old but not frayed. The carpet was deep, it sagged as she walked on it. There was an old iron heater on the other wall, closed behind a wrought iron frame. There were paintings of hillsides, cityscapes. She saw a painting of King Charles I, James' spoiled heir with his talk of the Divine Right of Kings. The other wall was taken up by a French window – wide enough for two people to walk through.

"Don't touch anything," the woman said. She left.

A single wooden beam ran along the room's entire length. Niamh tried to keep away from the middle of the room, lest she strike her head – the beam was a menace. The fireplace was unlit, the heater cold. It was Chorley in June and Niamh couldn't help but shiver.

A small bookcase held books as follows: Kelly's guides to Acton, Sudbury, and Wandsworth, the dates on their spines, 1906, 1924 and 1932. There was a London A to Z from 1953 with a pretty, yellow cover and a drawing of Nelson's column. Another shelf held a Yellow Pages from 1985. It was large, bulky, and worn by regular use. There were books by novelists that Niamh didn't know – Patrick Hamilton, Simon Blumenfeld – along with two London names she recognised – Peter Ackroyd and Iain Sinclair. Jake had put her onto them. Niamh took heart from the most recent books, reminded herself that several Sanden generations had made a home here. She could concentrate on the younger Sandens, use them against Teddy.

At last, the woman from earlier entered the room. "Her ladyship will be ten minutes," she said. She walked out again before Niamh could argue.

Niamh was alone once more. The room was still, silent. All the sounds came from outside, the lapping of water in the distance. The shrill cry of some large bird, a pheasant she supposed. Some instinct urged her to step back.

She was glad that she had when, without any warning, the French window opened from the outside. She saw again the man with the corrupted face. Into the room he came, wearing the same white shirt, the same sable ribbon and coal-dust hat as before. He shuffled in front of her. He grimaced as he moved. He was so close to her that Niamh could see the lines scored into his skin. He did not turn round, gave no sign of having noticed her. She took a step back and stared at him. He did not seem to notice or care. She said, "Excuse me."

He said, "It was here, it should be – it's got to be." He stood at his desk, a struggle of movement, then scrabbling in the drawer as if convinced it held an object he needed, something more important than the day, or the time, or her.

He searched again, raged with the fury of a rich person not used to being thwarted. "The Devil take them," he said, his thin lips crackling in frustration.

The wrinkled man reached for the drawer then thrust it backwards, sending the desk into the wall. The plaster was scored, was in fact already scored, showed a dozen indentations, more. Someone had scarred the plaster fifty times at least. He'd been there before, looked for the same lost item, been frustrated and overcome with anger. Not once, but many times before.

Niamh held herself as still as night. Her heart was as loud as a Lambeg drum. She'd met him once before and already she loathed him. She didn't dare speak.

The man shook for a moment, went still. He stared at her. "You seem familiar–"

"We've been introduced."

"The new cleaning girl?"

Niamh started to correct him, wilted in the glare of those two fierce eyes, then decided to play along. "Niamh, sir. I came up yesterday from London."

"About time too. The last one was worthless." He turned his face back to the desk, his neck twisting as slow as a cargo ship in water. "Where is it?"

"Where's what?"

"The coin," Sanden said, looking at the desk again, and she thought she saw in the opaque pools of his eyes not rage, but sorrow, a sadness so deep you could drown in it. He didn't start, or say anything, he showed no signs of recognising her voice. He was wrapped up in his own disappointment. He said, "The penny the hell-hag gave my daughter."

"I'm sorry, sir," she said, "I haven't seen it."

He nodded to himself, kept his eyes on the table. "Damn them all."

The old man left, exiting by the same French window through which he'd come. As he did, life returned to the room. The temperature rose. Birds could be heard once more chittering around the house. She let herself breathe. How could she let that wizened creature have such an effect on her? Niamh felt stupid, ashamed. She held a hand to her burning cheek.

And yet, nothing bad had happened to her. Her heart slowed. She waited. Her feet were tired, but she couldn't sit. She didn't dare, lest it was added to the list of her transgressions: approaching by a private road; trespassing; spying–-

At last, a different woman joined her in the room. "Xanthe Armstrong," she said, without offering a hand. The woman had blonde hair, brushed forwards over her head, and lacquered. It looked like someone had glued a yellow tiara to her head. Her skin was very pale. She wore a shooting vest, moleskin shoulder paddings, over a pair of white leggings. She was sixty at least, and, judging by the way she was shaking her head, the matriarch of the house.

"Niamh Malone."

"Well?" the woman demanded.

Well, what? Niamh wanted to answer, but she knew how weak her position was, and had determined to be polite. She beamed at the woman, "Pleased to meet you."

Mrs Armstrong said, "Come on, there's no use standing there, simpering at me. What are you doing in my house?"

"Your woman, what's her name–"

"Wallis?"

"She let me in." Niamh waited for an answer. Not getting one, she continued, "I'm a student in London, I've been researching your ancestors–"

"Without the least encouragement from any of us."

"I wrote," said Niamh.

"You didn't."

"It must have got lost in the post."

"I may look old to you, young woman, but let me reassure you of two things. First, I have a good memory. Second, our post is as dependable as a Cartier. When I say you never wrote, I mean – you didn't."

Niamh tried again, "What I wanted to ask is – can I speak to Teddy?"

The woman stared at her.

"Teddy, your relative?"

"I will be seventy-seven years old in September," Mrs Armstrong said. "Both my parents are dead. I don't have any siblings – nor children for that matter."

Niamh felt herself shrink. She knew how ridiculous her words seemed, but she was too far gone, she couldn't stop now. "He's your uncle, then."

As she spoke, another thought occurred to her. Teddy was short for Edward, wasn't it? He could in theory be the same Edward Sanden as had inhabited this building in the times of the Tudors. In a world which could produce superhuman water monsters, there must be space as well for immortal witchfinders, poets who were old beyond counting. She groaned. Edward had watched his children into their graves.

He'd terrified the villagers, with the result that they knew better than to say anything about him. She hated the idea, but it was possible, wasn't it? She remembered the old man she'd seen in Hector Sanden's last moments. Edward, Jenny had called him. *Oh God*, Niamh thought. She'd been so slow.

Teddy Sanden, Edward Sanden, the man in Hector's dream – all of them were the same man.

Mrs Armstrong was saying, "There is no circumstance in the world where I would allow a stranger into my house, making our lives a misery."

Niamh answered, "He was here a moment ago. He didn't seem that delicate."

"He's been on the estate all afternoon."

"I spoke to him."

"You can't have. He's been digging up ragwort in the fields. You can't have spoken to him. I don't know why you made it up, to humiliate me I suppose."

"He asked me where his coin had gone."

"Never," Mrs Armstrong said, "have I been insulted like this."

All right, thought Niamh, taking the rebuke as a challenge. "Ask the old man if I can speak to him. Let him decide."

Her hostess barked in frustration – like a cornered fox.

Had you told Niamh before she'd arrived that she would make a total mess of the occasion, she'd have felt embarrassed. She'd have blushed. Instead, she realised she was enjoying herself. She wondered if it was Jenny's bad influence. Her good influence.

Mrs Armstrong was shaking her head. "How could you? How dare you?"

The fury of Mrs Armstrong's reaction surprised Niamh, and she felt a need to placate her. She said, "All right, I don't know. I'll do whatever you want. Maybe–"

"If you keep on insulting me, I'll have to call the police."

"Call them," said Niamh, her brief willingness to help rapidly abating. "They don't scare me."

Mrs Armstrong seemed to wilt. She started to say something, she seemed to think the better of it. She said, "I'll ask him."

Then she beamed a little, shy smile – as if to say to Niamh that the two of them were both women, strong women, and why did they need to fight? "I can't have you speaking to Teddy today though, not the state he's in." Mrs Armstrong didn't call for the old man. Nor did she reach for her phone. "He's been so distracted, these past few days." She twisted from side to side, as if already regretting her decision. She said, "I don't know what I'll do with you, but one more word, and it'll be something terrible."

That night, Niamh slept behind a locked door. Mrs Armstrong's one real decision, as Niamh understood it, had been to defer what to do with her until the next morning. Wallis was making it clear that her mistress had let the other occupiers down. She glared as she led Niamh up the stairs, across the house, to her room. "This way," she said. "Keep up."

As they walked past empty rooms, Niamh was able to take in what seemed to her rooms full of expensive-looking furniture. In one chamber, there was another of those dark paintings, a city street, with the shadow of adults, and children on the pavement. As for her own room, it was plastered in drawings of butterflies. It had been a child's room, once. She wondered if Tom Sanden had learned to play his mandolin there, if Hector had grown up staring at the walls.

"Thank you," said Niamh. "It's cosy," she lied.

The door closed without answer.

She listened to the sounds coming from the corridor. For

long minutes, Wallis stood on the far side of the door, breathing her hatred of the house's unwanted guest. At last, she placed a key in the lock, turned it, trapping Niamh in the room.

"What if I need the toilet?"

"Do you need it now?"

"No."

"Then you can wait till the morning."

"What if I need food?"

When Walliss's footsteps withdrew, Niamh removed the bag from her back. That was her future: until the Sandens relented, she was their prisoner. She went to the window, stared out at the lake. The walls were vertical. The ground outside was a stone path. Sixty feet down, nothing to break her fall. She doubted she'd survive it.

She placed the tankard on the bedside table, said, "We're alone."

Niamh lifted its lid. She saw, to her dismay, that much of the valuable liquid had spilled on the journey. At the beginning of the day, it had been two-thirds full of water. Now, whether through evaporation or her carelessness, no more than three fingers of the vital elixir remained.

"I didn't mean to waste it," she said.

Thou didst hand me like a whirligig, she imagined Jenny complaining.

She thought, for a moment, of repeating her friend's name. Say it loud in summoning. But this wasn't the time. Although Niamh had the power of calling Jenny, she had no spell for sending Jenny back again afterwards. She thought of Liam, how little he'd deserved the harm that Niamh and Jenny had done him. She hadn't forgotten Hector. If she called on Jenny now, her companion would demand revenge. She would attack Teddy, Mrs Armstrong, Wallis too. Niamh distrusted the women who protected the house, but that was the limit of her ill-feeling towards them, a mere shallow dislike. If Jenny was to kill them, that would be Niamh's fault. Better to wait and see if an opportunity presented itself.

Niamh said, "I know you're listening. Give me a day, let me see what I can find out. That's all I'm asking for. One day, all right?"

She waited.

Choosing to treat silence as assent, she put the lid back on the tankard.

She looked on the shelves, which hadn't been dusted, saw illustrated books, how-to guides to hunting and fishing. Another volume was older and didn't have an author's name on its spine. Bound in a soft leather, it held several passages. The extracts had been transcribed in a neat hand, each letter spaced apart from its neighbour, with commentary added in the margin where the copyist had slipped. There was nothing to distinguish its title or its owner, save for two initials on the inside cover – and two significant ones: "E. S."

Niamh smiled in recognition. Sanden. Had to be,

She read on. The first few pages held drawings of pikemen in formation. Soldiers with their muskets, patterns for marching troops.

On another page, a series of drawings had been made, triangles marked in an antique hand. As, and Bs, and Cs, 30°, 60°, 90°. Euclidean triangles.

She read on, hoping that the book would hold some clue to the old man who dominated the house. She was hoping to find a lost poem but the remaining pages were empty.

Niamh lay on the bed. She listened to the sounds of water, dripping through antique pipes. She was too hot beneath the covers. She missed the city, the sound of cars whooshing along the roads in the distance. How easy it would be to imagine something – a physical presence – into the room. She switched the light off.

She refused to give herself nightmares.

She hid, hating to think what creatures were out there, wriggling through the darkness. She kept her head on the pillow and her eyes closed.

CHAPTER 14
BITTER DISCOVERY

When the door opened, the next morning, Mrs Armstrong gave no apology for having locked Niamh in overnight. "Come with me," she said, and she marched her guest downstairs. The words rattled out of her, "Great Hall. Reception room. Guest suite," as if Niamh was a welcome visitor being granted the honour of a formal tour rather than the interloper which she was, liable to be thrown out at any moment. "Entertaining room," Mrs Armstrong told her, allowing Niamh to see a room with a heavy, beamed ceiling and a floor which gleamed with polish. Three armchairs sat beyond a fireplace, each with cushions that looked new, unyielding. Niamh tried to imagine anyone entertaining there, it was all too clean – antiseptic.

"Do you mind I sit on one of the sofas?" said Niamh.

"Please don't," her hostess said. "Not in your jeans."

For breakfast, there was toast and watery marmalade, and Niamh liked marmalade. She asked if she could speak to Teddy. Her hostess was in a benevolent mood but wouldn't give her a straight answer.

Mrs Armstrong was going out. She was wearing a lah-di-dah hat, blue, all ribbons, a blue-painted rose held in place with a pin. She was going to the shops, Niamh suspected. But keeping up appearances. Because that's what the Sandens did, didn't they?

"Teddy gets these fits," Mrs Armstrong was saying. "Terrible things. In summer, they can last for days, but he gets through them in the end."

Niamh said, "It must be awful having to look after him–"

Mrs Armstrong lifted her hands and smiled a complicit smile.

"But can I speak to him? That's all I want."

"I've asked him."

"What did he say?"

"He's agreed to meet you."

"When?"

Mrs Armstrong looked up, her eyes red and tired – defeated. The woman said, "Tell me. How's London at this time of year?"

"London?"

"All of it, the shops, the streets. I want you to tell me it's glorious in Piccadilly in night-time. If you still see couples going arm in arm as they enter the Ritz?"

"I guess," said Niamh, who'd never gone inside the Ritz. Or any of the other tourist-traps that Mrs Armstrong remembered.

"You're so lucky to live somewhere busy. If you wanted to, you could have culture every night – theatre, ballet. It's all on your doorstep."

"That's true, I guess." Niamh was conscious of how little of the city she'd explored. She knew Pimlico and the King's Road from Vron, had spent evenings in Islington with her friends, but most of zone one was no better a hazy, white expanse filled by a street here, a junction there. She'd never been to Park Lane, let alone Mayfair.

"What are people wearing, this year?"

Niamh didn't trust Mrs Armstrong's *people*, but, knowing that some answer was expected of her, Niamh stammered out some inconsequential response. Something about how her girlfriends were wearing black. What she wanted to say was that they wore what their parents wore. That was what had happened to culture; you had all the same styles on hard repeat, punk, hippy, techno, a record spinning round.

She said, "I like your hat."

Xanthe lifted a hand to her blue armour. "This? It's been in the family forever."

The meal ended without any clear answer as to when Niamh would meet Sanden.

After breakfast, Niamh went out. She wanted to explore the area outside of Sanden Hall. There wasn't much more than a house, a garden, a large glass-house made up of a series of small bushes, covered by a white wooden frame. Searching past the outhouses, she found them in a state of decay, their wooden doors chained, the padlocks rusting in the damp June air. Once, the Hall had been much busier than it was now, a workplace employing several dozen people. She imagined Edward Sanden on a high-backed chair. She could see him younger, bearded, ticking off the points of some lecture he was giving his wife while the poor woman watched, her face cast down in mute deference, her daughters hugging her skirts.

Niamh was tired. She hated the building. It was as if the house was alive, leering, polluting all it touched. She should never have let Jenny talk her into coming. She sat by the reservoir, watching the light play upon the water. Ducks swam near the shore. The day was cold, as if autumn had arrived two months too soon. Mist hugged the ground, the clouds gathered above her. She sat on a wooden log, half-awake, half-asleep, with no desire to return to the butterfly room. The sky clouded, then darkened further.

There was an electric feeling in the air as if with all this pressure, rain would come, and soon. Dampness clustered between the trees, the gloom deepened. Niamh clung the arms of her sweater around her. Thicker and thicker, the clouds congregated.

Lunch was hours away and yet the day was as dark as night.

As she sat in the gloom, Niamh saw something moving above the water. She remembered how the reservoir had been made – it hadn't always been water here. The shape approached at speed, revealed itself to be an open carriage, with a white horse at the front. With a clatter of hooves, the vehicle stopped. From it, six women stepped down. Two were older women. One was wearing a peasant smock, carrying a basket in one hand, a stick in another. A hood covered her head. The sleeves hung long. Two of the women were middle-aged, stout, in russet dresses. They held their heads bowed. The last two were younger, children. The movements of all the women became rapid, full of joy. They embraced one another.

They pointed at the Sanden home – laughed at its inhabitants.

In that moment, Niamh knew what she was seeing: the shades of the six accused women. Not those villagers from the present-day who'd been given the task of re-enacting their trial, but the women themselves, as if brought back to life. They'd feared the assize, had lived in terror of what Sanden might say, but the first day of the trial had gone well. The women had spoken there with a remarkable confidence. The old man in his big master's house had overreached himself. They wanted him to see their contempt for him.

A younger Jenny walked among them. Unmistakeable in her black dress. Her smile gleaming through the darkness, she laughed alongside her co-accused. She held her companions in her arms. "Sister, thou didst well," said this shadow-Jenny from the past. Niamh remembered a passage from one of Sanden's poems. The poet had been mourning the rule of King James, praising the old curmudgeon's skill in preventing danger. Spanish intrigues, the threat posed by tobacco, by witchcraft. During his long praise-poem, Sanden had written a couplet which escaped the bounds of the stale laudations around it:

"All their arrogant pleasures come to this,
They gossip as they prepare to descend the great Abyss."

And that, Niamh thought, had been Sanden's fantasy all along. The myth of divine approval. The Puritans had believed it, too. If they couldn't make the women obey, then God would punish them, make them burn in Hell for all Eternity. Or, the next best thing, a jury selected of male householders would convict. The Crown, acting on God's authority, would punish them. Except it wasn't going to plan. The villagers hadn't done what they were meant to do. They had listened to the women. So far, the people believed them.

Niamh found herself remembering the confidence with which Margaret Waite had spoken. Niamh had always thought of Jenny's rebirth as some kind of opportunity, her chance to be revenged on the man who'd wronged her. But what if the women had been believed? What if, in speaking up for themselves, they'd exposed the limits of his power, and, at the height of the trial, he was the one who had no choice but to hide in his house, ashamed?

Niamh looked at the spirits, their smiles, their laughter. They were not victims. They had defied the village tyrant.

The storm broke. For an hour, rain fell, sleet clattered on the glass. Darkened the ground on which the apparitions stood, without removing them.

Back inside the house, Niamh couldn't stop thinking of the women. Niamh was still remembering them when Wallis summoned her to lunch. Outside, it was cold and wet, and the blinds had been drawn in the kitchen. Behind Mrs Armstrong, a line of copper pans hung down from the beams. A dozen black knife-handles extended from a wooden block. One of them sat on a carving board in front of her, large and heavy.

"My dad used to carve our Sunday dinners," said Niamh, feeling stupid as soon as she'd shared the memory. But it was true. He'd kept a steel and sharpened the blade before the Sunday meal. Her mum must had thrown out all his things when he left.

"Hector carved for us," her hostess said.

Niamh swallowed. She felt for an awful moment as if she'd been discovered.

"He stayed in London. I had to come back for Teddy."

Niamh couldn't force herself to ask who Hector was.

The conversation returned to London. Mrs Armstrong began asking about areas: Lincoln's Inn. Gray's Inn Road. Did Niamh know them? Did she have any friends living there or thereabouts? What were the shops like?

Niamh squeezed her hands together, ground her nail into the skin beneath her thumb. Mrs Armstrong seemed to believe that England was still a country in which one per cent of all eighteen-year-olds went to university, that she and her contemporaries were going to be internet millionaires, when, in ten years, she expected her friends to have jobs which wouldn't pay the interest on their student dent. She wasn't *one of them*, no matter what Mrs Armstrong thought.

Mrs Armstrong said she had spoken to Edward. "I told him you were a student. From London. Come to learn about the history of the house. Cheered him up like anything."

"He agreed to meet me?"

"I persuaded him." Mrs Armstrong's voice softened, and for a moment Niamh could see behind the barriers the old woman had built, the younger, freer person Mrs Armstrong had once been when she didn't own the house or its responsibilities. "He likes it when he has visitors, it's so unusual these days. You'll be his captive audience."

"Not too captive, I hope. Can we speak – this afternoon?"

"Teddy and summer don't get on. He gets these terrible headaches. So, not today, he's in no fit state. But I'll ask again, tomorrow."

Niamh went back to her room and tried to read. The interview with Sanden seemed to be coming closer, which was a relief, but the details were still vague. The rain was continuing to fall. She lay on her back, twisted onto her side. She turned round and lay with her feet on the pillow. She tried the chair by the bed, she tried the floor. She brought out Malone. Arthur, and the last of his men. Wounded they were after the merfolks' attack, but still they lived. So long as they did, there was hope for England. She stood by the window, watched the reservoir outside, what happened to the surface of the liquid as the rain fell on it, was absorbed by it, as if the water was thick, viscous, like plastic or molten glass.

She took the tankard out of the backpack and placed it on the table beside her. She told the pewter mug, the cold, white, damp, and empty room, "I can't stand this place, I want to go back. I've had enough. It's so creepy here. Every time I walk past a mirror, I'm looking in the corners, wondering if there's something trapped in them, trying to get out."

I will come to thee now.

"No, that's not what I'm saying. I don't want you here, I want to go home." The day was cold, the afternoon dark. Her request was in all ways a reasonable one.

Didst thou see Sanden?

"I did, kind of. I will."

I will come there now.

"Don't," said Niamh. "I'm telling you, don't harm them – I won't allow it."

Didst thou speak to him?

"For a moment. It wasn't the right time for your purposes. But I'm going to see him again, with proper warning next time. As soon as I know when, I'll tell you."

Niamh and Jenny were supposed to be allies. Yet here she was, ordering the woman about. "I'm sorry," she said. "I know how much this matters to you, and I won't muck it up. You must believe me, if you get here too soon, you'll ruin everything."

She took the silence of the room as a reluctant vote of confidence.

Niamh didn't want to spend the afternoon by the reservoir, she needed an excuse for a longer walk. She remembered Sister Isidore in the next-door village. The nun was free, and answered her text the moment it was sent, saying yes, she'd love to meet. The walk was an easy one, a gentle upward climb through grass fields glistening like jewels.

It was still daylight when Niamh arrived. Isidore's house seemed to Niamh the sort of property at which a Miss Marple should live, set back from the road, with roses in the garden, two white-painted steel chairs. It wasn't the biggest house in the district, but the garden was one which could keep its owner busy all through the summer. Niamh had been looking forward to meeting Isidore's daughter, but the woman was resting.

As she and the Sister chatted, there was a sadness at the edge of Isidore's words, and Niamh wondered what it must be like, for a woman who had been all her years smart, sardonic, in a village which put no weight on either of those virtues.

"I'm not keeping you from her, am I?" Niamh asked.

"No, not at all. She sees the world in different hues to everyone else. Some days, she can do with a little help. Other days, she guards her independence."

Niamh sighed. "You don't get in the way?"

"There would be no point if I tried. Lucy is a woman of strong opinions, bless her. I would no more waste my time trying to persuade her against a path on which she was set, than would I complain about the Chorley weather. You can't fight nature."

"I've not encountered many mothers who respect their daughter's boundaries."

Silence.

Niamh said, "Then again, I've not spent much time with a nun before."

Judging by the smile on Sister Isidore's face, this was an easier topic of conversation. "We don't bite."

"I get that. And I'm so glad I've got someone to talk to."

The sun was low in the sky before the conversation turned to Niamh, and her progress. "You're still researching our lords and masters, I take it," Isidore said.

"Something like that. Trying to."

"I had hoped you might be planning a longer holiday, a few days here at least."

"I'll need to get home at some point," said Niamh.

"But the Sandens are helping you?"

"They've let me stay with them, which is more than I could have expected."

"Found out anything wicked?" Isidore looked at Niamh. Many things about her were old, but not her eyes. They were as blue as the sea on a summer's day.

"Not much." For a painful moment, Niamh wondered if she was disappointing the old woman. She said, "I've found a man who looks like he's walked out of his own grave and, apart from you and his niece – if that's what she is – everyone else pretends that it isn't anything remarkable to have a 400-year-old zombie in their lives."

Isidore said, "When the followers of King Charles I went hunting for the regicides, most were already dead. In at least one case, they exhumed the body of the man they considered a traitor. When they cut into the corpses, blood seeped out as it would from a living man. The supporters of the King declared that God had preserved the bodies so that they might undergo further punishment, even after death. To keep him from coming back, they stuck Oliver Cromwell's head on a spike and showed it to the crowds at Westminster. They called themselves Christian but their fear of the afterlife made them a crowd of pagans."

"I don't get it. You're saying that the people were right to fear the undead? You're telling me I should believe in zombies?"

"It's years, Niamh, since I told anyone what to think. What I'm saying, I suppose, is that the Sandens employ half the village. People don't dare stand up to them."

"How convenient for Edward."

"He doesn't get things all his own way. They know that he's beyond rational explanation. They aren't stupid, he's a thing of wonder to them – and shame too. They know not to breathe a word about him to strangers. To that extent he's protected, but he still can't go anywhere. There are too many people out there who might ask tough questions. Food must be delivered. Whenever it comes in, he's always making himself scarce."

"It's more freedom than he deserves."

"But they're speaking to you?"

"His niece says I'm going to meet him. Tomorrow, I

suppose."

"You're telling me the Sandens have reformed? After fifty years of hiding from strangers, they've made an exception for you?"

"A half-exception," said Niamh, smiling at herself, to think how large her grievances had seemed in Sanden Hall, and how small they seemed when she was with Isidore.

Her hostess reached into her pocket, extracted a pack of red Dunhill's. She lit one, kept the cigarette at a polite distant from Niamh. She said, "You know, the thing that always puzzles me about this place is why didn't it ever grow up? Why did they leave the nobs in charge? You travel about England, and there were all sorts of people in the villages. Coal-mining, for decades, their union shook the countryside up. In the sixties, there was alternative religion, the Campaign for Nuclear Disarmament. At one time, it was quite the most fashionable thing to declare your hamlet a nuclear-free zone. In other places, it was young people running away from London. Here, though, they had none of that. Nothing changed, no one dared complain about the Sandens. We left them where they always were, at the heart of village life. Even the water we drink, it all comes from their lake."

"So how did your daughter end up here?"

Sister Isidore looked back towards the house, then bent forward. "An unsuitable marriage," she said, wrinkling her nose as if teasing herself. "But don't you dare tell her I said that. He was a thief, a handsome and a charming rogue."

"Did she stand up to him?"

"She intended to, started to, met with a lawyer. Various family members tried to help, did help. It's hard, though, finding the strength to leave someone who's abused you."

"She wanted to fight?"

"She did, for a time. And then it seemed to her that there

was no point, that even by thinking of him, she was still under his control. Even to recover such little strength as she has now, even that was a battle. The first step would have been to forget him. Even that, I'm afraid, was beyond her power."

"I'm so sorry."

Isidore sucked on her cigarette, then stubbed it on the ashtray. "I don't know what you're trying to do to the Sanden. Whatever it is, you won't find it easy. I've seen the old man and, you're right, he's not much of a looker, is he? I remember the first time I met him, it wasn't long after I'd moved in. A man out of time, with his face rotting away. If we were nearer to Liverpool, to Manchester, someone would have stood up to him by now. I'm telling you, if my daughter wasn't lumbered with her unsellable house, I'd have moved her a hundred miles to get away from him. I've seen him since, in the village, more than once, and–"

"Where?" asked Niamh, "Where does he go?"

"The inn, as you've seen. Sanden Hall. Then there's St. Andrew's, it was the family church. They had a pew – he's always patrolling the graveyard."

"I haven't been to St Andrew's," said Niamh, making a mental note.

"I was there a week ago. He had me thrown out," Isidore said. "That's when I realised. I always thought he scared me, but I could see it was mutual."

Niamh said. "He's a zombie."

"That's the third time you've called him that, but he's nothing of the sort. Zombies aren't real. Nor are vampires, nor skeletons."

"Then what is he?"

The nun shrugged.

"You don't believe in magic, do you?"

"Not in the least," Isidore told her.

"But wasn't that part of what the Church used to do? I read somewhere – Like, in the middle ages, if there was some cult about a person who'd died in some mysterious way, the Church was always thinking, 'Can't we make him a saint?' Or relics, weren't there so many so bits of wood from the Holy Cross that you could build a galley out of them?"

"You're saying that religion is magic?"

"No, but didn't religion borrow from magic, copy it in places?"

The Sister shook her head, "Truth and superstition were ever antagonists. Religion didn't borrow from magic, we didn't. If anything, it was the other way around. When they discovered Christianity, the Romans were in awe. The Fathers used to record with astonishments the lies that were told about us. The Romans slandered them, said the followers of Jesus ate the flesh of children and called it bread. They said that, in our Communion, we drank blood. And those rumours – they hung around. In later generations, foolish people, wicked people, thought they could buy some power by making those old slanders real. They cut the throats of their victims, tried to drink the blood before it coagulated. But there were many other kinds of magic, little humdrum things. The poor would go to church and listen to a priest speak in Latin and tell themselves that if they repeated some nonsense with the same slow voice then the words themselves would have a power. *Pater Noster, qui es in caelis, abracadabra*. The rich too. They heard the wind and confused it for God's own tears. They believed words were magic. Any words."

Niamh blushed, "I'm sorry, I didn't mean to attack the things you believe in." The Sister's answer, the solemn way in which she'd taken the question, had left her feeling very foolish. "Maybe I've been listening too much to superstition," she said.

"Faith has sustained you too, I believe. That cross I gave you."

"That was your faith. It helped me for a bit – and then it didn't anymore."

"I have other crosses. Take one, you could treat it as a gift from the foolish creature that I am, an old mother, to a much smarter younger woman."

"It's fine," Niamh said.

"It would put my mind at rest, to think of you protected."

"Why don't you come back with me? We could confront him together. I'm starting to think you might be my best chance."

"Niamh Malone," the sister said. "I am seventy-six years old. I walk with a limp, which most people don't see, but it's there you'd better believe me. I have arthritis, neuropathy. I wouldn't be any use in a monster hunt. I'm sorry but I wouldn't be."

"I'm an atheist," Niamh said. "On the way here, I thought I needed an artefact. A rosary, baptism water. I'd borrow it from you. Or I'd go into the Sanden sheds, find wood and hammer and sharpen myself a stake. It was a daft idea–"

"Why call it that?"

"I don't know, it seems so – melodramatic. I mean, he's not a ghost, not a vampire. He's nothing more than an old man–"

"Sustained by contempt," the nun said.

The two women sat for a moment. Niamh was enjoying the dusky evening, the fact of the older woman's company. Isidore, too, was smiling.

"I was intending to give you some advice," the Sister said at last. "Although it's sounds like it's something you've worked out already for yourself. There isn't any trick that's going to solve all your problems, there never is. The answer, whatever it is, is inside you."

On her return to Sanden Hall, Wallis sighed as she let Niamh in, did not offer her food. The house was silent, the curtains closed. Niamh felt she had no choice but to retreat to her room. There, she waited. Of Jenny's liquid, a mere inch remained. She sat by the chair, with the view of the window. She thought of London.

Niamh said out loud, "If I go to St. Andrews, will you come with me?"

If she'd been expecting a sudden flash of light – a happening, an incarnation – she was disappointed. The room remained empty.

"All right," Niamh said, "You win, I'm staying. Are you happy now?"

Niamh waited.

She turned to her books and looked for solace in them.

When her eyes opened, it was one in the morning. Niamh had always taken pride in how well she slept. Put her on the back seat of a car, and four times out of five she'd be asleep before the vehicle found the main road. A mere sagging mattress was no hardship to her. She'd managed to keep up her record of deep sleeping all the way through university, despite her landlady's midnight soirees, her habit of playing Oliva Newton John when Niamh was trying to sleep. Now, here she was deep in the countryside, and the few sounds coming through the walls were the wind in the trees, the pleading of sparrows. She should have slept like a stone.

These were some of the tricks that Niamh tried in the attempt to send herself back to sleep. She lay on her back, on her front, on her side.

She picked up her book, reached for the light, thought the better of it. She threw herself on her side again, the darkness all around her. The pillow felt thin beneath her cheek. She imagined locking her body in this position, as if by making herself still she'd rest.

The blanket was so heavy. Niamh twisted in the bed. Any moment now and she'd sleep. Any moment– She could hear footsteps, slow and heavy in the corridor. Niamh's heart sped up. She could feel the tension in her stomach. *Hey*. She made her arms, and body relax. *Hey*, she told herself, *it's all right. Go back to sleep, and you'll be fine*.

The steps retreated; the corridor was silent.

Niamh saw light pulsing in through the window. She twisted away, turned back. She sat upwards, made herself stare out into the air, the lake, as if by confronting the presence – whatever it was – it would have no choice to but to leave her. There was no light. She saw the trees in the distance, the great belt of them which swaddled the edge of the lake. Niamh shivered. She pulled at the blanket, but it did not give. She thought of going to the window, of running out into the corridor but she could imagine the glee with which Wallis would report her fear to her mistress: *The girl, ma'am, She's afraid of her own shadow. I saw her, with my own eyes, running into the corridor.* Niamh didn't want anyone talking about her, she wouldn't give them the excuse. She sank down beneath the covers.

She heard fingers drumming on the door. Niamh wouldn't look, she didn't dare, but she knew what she'd see if she looked. Sanden's hideous face, his eye glinting through the keyhole. Tap-tap-tap, the fingers searching for a way in.

Niamh knew he was coming and she was in danger. She told herself that the door was strong, she'd checked it before going to bed. *Calm down calm down calm down*. The dull tapping sound ceased, was replaced with something new – a pecking sound like a bird hunting for worms. The creature was picking at the lead beneath the handle. Something metal fell to the floor. Cold forced its way in. Niamh didn't want to be there. She closed her eyes, her arms and shoulders squeezed tight in hatred. Her body was in agony.

She wasn't afraid, *she wasn't afraid.* She hadn't seen anything to scare her, but her heart was restless, and her chest tight. It was her mind playing tricks on her.

The room was silent.

Silent.

Silent.

"I don't believe in ghosts," she told the room – told Sanden. He was there beside her.

Wake up, she urged herself – without moving.

She tried to make herself move but she was too weak. He loomed over the side of the bed, his wrinkles deep in his withered yellow skin.

He reached his long, bony fingers down. He twisted them in her hair. Up they lifted and down they came again. With terrible slowness, he gripped her neck. His hands were so cold, they burned her skin. His wrists turned. She could feel the pressure. She tried to fight but was held in invisible iron chains. Closer his face came – his mouth close enough to kiss.

Now his lips were upon her. There was a light catching squeak of a sound, like a child sucking upon a straw. She could feel the breath being extracted from her chest.

She couldn't move. The room swam in front of her. She couldn't move. The pain in her chest was unbearable. She remembered Hector.

He let go. Her head fell to the pillow.

"So rich with life," he said.

Sanden was enjoying himself. The lines on his face, which

had been mountains and valleys, smoothed. Some tentative colour had returned to his cheeks.

Down he bent once more, his skin pink, restored.

Niamh fought like she'd never fought before – raged, and *somehow* – broke free from the spell holding her. She twisted her head to one side. She screamed, but the sound was so weak, a broken fury.

Sanden took a reluctant step back away from the bed.

Niamh writhed, kicked, sucked in what air she could down her narrowed windpipes. She croaked, "Get out!"

He stared at her – as astonished as she was to see her move.

Niamh couldn't do this on her own. "Jenny," she sobbed. "You will come in my need."

The air shimmered. The creature was inside in the room. Jenny swayed to balance, as if she'd been dragged away from some other business – and struggled to find her footing.

"You're here," Niamh whimpered. Her chest spasming, she rolled out of the bed, crawled with joy towards her friend. But she received no welcoming gesture, no words of thanks. The woman was in battle-mode, staring at Edward. "Thou liv'st!"

The old man answered, "As you do too. For many years I wanted to see you one last time. For a time beyond counting, I waited."

"Waited?" Jenny spat the word. "Exulted, more like."

"Any harm I did to you," Edward says, "was returned to me double. I was bereaved of mine own children. I was made to live beyond any time that nature allows. Why need'st you trouble me, when you have had your vengeance already?"

"I have had no justice." She shoved him – hard – in the chest.

Edward stepped back, bent at the waist, absorbed the

force of her blow.

Jenny howled in frustration.

Round the room, the two fighters twisted, Niamh crawling behind Jenny. "We can do this," Niamh wheezed, tried to stand, collapsed back against the wall.

Jenny hissed, waved her away. *Leave this to me.*

Niamh reached for Sanden's commonplace book, flung it at him. It arced up to waist high, flopped to the ground beside him.

Facing Jenny, the old man said, "You should have stayed in Hell. When you have returned there, Beelzebub himself will tear your soul upon his rack."

"I would endure all harms, Edward, to see thee punished beside me."

Jenny attacked. She fainted with her left hand. Then, when Sanden parried, she punched her right hand into his sword-fist, sending the weapon clattering to the floor. "Nature has given me dominion," she said, "over all brazen men."

Sanden looked at his sword and smiled. "But not over me."

Jenny shaped her fingers into claws. "Monster, thou shalt die."

Sanden sneered. "You are not strong enough."

"While age has made thou chary."

"Do not confuse caution for weakness." A blur of movement, he bent down, grabbed his sword. Forward, he thrust.

She dodged once more.

Another step to the side, and Sanden was by the window, by the table. He lifted the tankard which held the last of the London water. He poured it to the ground. "None of your witchcraft this time," he said. He leered a horrible grin.

Jenny flinched, "There was none before, you hare-brained fool."

Sanden lifted once more the sword. He forced his enemy backwards. Then charging with a speed impossible in one so old, he pushed up with his other hand, catching Jenny's jaw, pushed her backwards. She raged and fought without escaping from his grasp.

"Lord have mercy on your soul." He thrust his sword into Jenny's stomach.

Niamh cried out. She could see blood on her companion's dress, blood on Sanden's blade. "You bastard," she sobbed.

Again, the man stabbed Jenny. The blood flowered down her shirt. Then, with a triumphant lurch of his shoulders, he pushed her to the ground.

Sanden paused for breath. He leered down at her. "To Hell, wench."

Jenny whispered, "This – it shall not avail thee."

Out, Sanden pulled his weapon. Into her chest, he thrust it once more. Blood flooded out in a weak rebuke against is blade. A rage of jubilant fury moved him. Niamh screamed at him to shop. She flung herself at him.

"She's dead – already." The words broke in Niamh's mouth.

Sanden pushed her away. He was standing over Jenny as the blood bubbled upwards out of her throat. Again, Sanden stabbed his sword into her chest. Withdrew it.

"You shit," Niamh said.

"My own friend that woman was, before she was to me a foe. I will honour her passing, bury her with reverence. Not in a pauper's plot, but in sanctified ground. Hush child, and ask yourself, would she have done the same for me?"

Niamh screamed again, threw herself at his face. Fighting, flailing her nails, but she could land no blow on him. He laughed, as she struggled, as she scratched her fingers without reaching his face. Niamh sobbed, as Sanden dragged

Jenny's lifeless body from the room.

CHAPTER 15
DOUBTING EVERYTHING

When Niamh woke, there was a nasty, sweet taste in her mouth. She supposed she must have bitten her tongue in the night. She left the bed, looked around the room – and, as she did, she remembered. From the bed, at the far corner of the room, she could see everything out of place. Her clothes trampled on. Her book discarded – its pages scattered. A mess of red smears on the wall. She saw the streaks on the wooden floor, where Sanden had dragged Jenny's corpse. The ground lurched beneath Niamh. She had to hold the wall to stop herself from falling. She spoke Jenny's name, begged to her. For long minutes, she could do nothing more than cry. Then, at last, she found some strength. She could not have explained where it came from, this incomprehensible determination to keep on going, but she went among her things, picked up her clothes, her tears dripping on the floor as she worked. The tankard of London water had been knocked to the side. Its contents were gone. "You're alive," Niamh whispered to herself, "you must be." But even as spoke the words out loud, she knew them to be a lie. She found the mirror. She saw the blue bruises of Sanden's fingers on her neck.

She filled the vessel with water from the tap. She tore up an old t-shirt to make rags. She took the liquid and used it to clean the wall, wash the floor. It was a long, slow, thankless task, and worse still in her weakened physical condition but better than leaving the room, better than seeing Wallis or

Mrs Armstrong doing it. Better to hide, to mourn and remember alone. She thought of Jenny, her second loss of the year. She uttered a silent prayer for Liam.

Breakfast was a small plate of scrambled eggs. By the time Wallis had led Niamh to her seat, Mrs Armstrong was up, finished, and already making herself her second cup of coffee of the morning. "Have you got any plans for the day?" Niamh's host said.

"I won't be leaving without seeing your uncle."

Mrs Armstrong's faced twisted. "I've told you before. If he's well, that's fine. But you wouldn't want to see him when he's in one of his moods."

"The thing is," Niamh continued, although her head spun with fatigue, "I'm so grateful to you for letting me stay. It's been wonderful, but there are things I need to do in London. So, it would help me if I could see him sooner rather than later. This morning, or I'm leaving."

"He's a very old man," Mrs Armstrong insisted.

"I need to get back to London," Niamh insisted. "Now. It can't wait."

"I'll see what I can do."

After breakfast, the stairs back to her room were an ordeal.

On her return, the bedroom was in surprising order. It smelled of water, of stale blood. The bed though – all of Niamh's things – were back where they needed to be. Niamh had forgotten how hard she'd worked that morning. She'd done better tidying up than she had any right to do, her body bursting with tiredness, her feet swollen, her hands sore. What use could she be if she was to confront Sanden now; how was she supposed to kill him if Jenny couldn't do it? But she needed to – had to before she collapsed with exhaustion.

The wheezing sound outside was Wallis. "His lordship's asked for you."

Doubting everything

Niamh said she needed a moment to herself. She made herself look, once more, upon the wooden floor, recall the sight of Jenny's corpse, remember the red blotches which had been left behind, the last remnants of her friend.

Their meeting – she would fight him, be revenged for Jenny's sake.

She returned to the drawing room. Sanden sat in his chair, as still as winter.

"You wanted to see me."

From the sofa, the old man rose. He stretched out a creaking arm, as if to introduce himself for the first time. He looked at her, sat back down again.

In his voice like broken gravel, Sanden said, "I have spoken to Xanthe. She tells me you came here from London."

"What's it to you?" Niamh was looking about the room, wondering if the old man kept the sword he'd used against Jenny. It wasn't anywhere to be seen.

"My granddaughter lived in the city. She misses it."

Niamh was looking for another weapon. The fire-tongs she thought, but they were blunt. "You collect books about London, don't you?"

"I have long wondered what it must be like to live in the city. My descendant Xanthe was there, in her youth, and we have discussed how it feels to live in a world larger than our own. The metropolis is a wonder even now."

"I suppose."

"When I was young, it held all the great treasures of the realm."

Niamh's plan had been a violent attack, the element of surprise. But she was being dragged into a conversation – one which displeased her.

She thought of the delayed trains, the towns outside London with their boarded-up shop windows. "Why now?

You could have gone there any time."

"Not true," he said. "Until this last week, my labours were always incomplete. A force beyond my control kept me to this district, made me the prisoner of its lanes and fields. Things now are changing, are continuing to change. It is as if I've always had a ball chained to my feet and, with the departure of your friend, the key was delivered by which I might unlock the chain. My work is almost done. One more night, and I shall be free."

Niamh glared at him, thought of dashing her empty fists on his face. She remember the night before, though, the ease with which he'd disposed of Jenny.

"Won't you congratulate me on obtaining my liberty?"

"I'm sure it's very gratifying."

"I could do with help. Someone to scope the city for me. Check to make sure that my family's envisaged accommodation is suitable. When all preparations are in order, my assistant would be rewarded. The Sandens are no misers."

Niamh's laugh was bitter. "They have solicitors for that."

The yellow gleam in Sanden's eyes made Niamh feel sick in her heart, in her stomach, all the way down to her shoes. Then his eyes glazed. He said, in a business-like tone, "You want to know about my ancestor. The coincidence of our names."

So that was how he was going to play it.

"The poet," said Niamh. But her heart wasn't in Sanden's game. This monster had killed Jenny. She had to fight him, but even as she accepted that task, urged it on herself, she shrank from it. She was too weak for the task.

"My predecessor suffered an unfortunate fate. I've mulled his story for many years–"

For four hundred years, and you expect me to play the innocent.

"Witches attacked him. I know it's hard to believe in them, but they're real."

"You say so," said Niamh, hating Sanden with every fibre of her being.

"My ancestors have guarded the story of the trial through centuries. On what basis could we be mistaken?"

She said, "I've researched it – I've – I've found everything there is. It's all online now, the records of every assize."

"If you know everything there is to find out already – then why did you bother me?" When she didn't answer, he continued. "What you need to understand," he said, "was that there were six women accused. There was Margaret Waite, a widow. Her husband had died already at the hand of the executioner. While Jennifer Gill had been a witch for many a long year–"

Niamh said, "I was in the hall. I heard your speech."

She waited for him to fight her. She expected him to continue the fiction that he was nothing more than a descendant of the first Edward Sanden. Pretend that nothing had happened between them. Ignore Jenny's death.

"Tell me, why did you come here?" he asked.

"Today? To kill you."

"Well, that is admirably blunt"

"I came for Jenny."

"Who has passed away." He spoke the words as if it was the most unfortunate thing, as if death had happened to Jenny, as if he wasn't the one who'd killed her.

"Why did you accuse the women?"

"They assailed my daughters with demons. They brought into my house strange animals, deformed things, cats black in colour with too many feet, white cats spotted in black."

"So, you believed it all – sticking pins in dolls?"

"I guarded my family from their enemies."

Niamh felt she should press him about his story. There would be something in the narrative, a clue, which she might use against him later. She wasn't ever going to be as strong as Jenny. Words, though. Words might be the answer. But the effort of stringing him along was beyond her. She said, "You make me sick–"

"Then leave. I will put no obstacle in your path."

"It didn't happen like that," Niamh said, squeezing her fists with the effort of fighting him. "All you had in front of you was a group of women, villagers with a broomstick in their kitchen. Your own fantasies were enough for you."

"I saw witches."

She said, "I imagine your wife spoke in a kind voice to Margaret Waite, and you didn't like it when the old woman smiled back. You thought she'd embarrassed you. You thought Meg wanted power over your household – when she wanted to be left alone, same as all the others. So, you wrote down your story, made your daughter memorise it so she could testify."

"They had a church. All the froth and scum of the villages attended it. I went to one of their services. They let a maid preach. She said that God was in all creatures. Her words were a libel on Christianity, a lunatic theory, a compound of iniquity and impudence. She made them enemies to God, to their own husbands, to themselves."

The two of them sat there for a while, scowling. The wind scraped against the walls of Sanden Hall, dry and joyless. Niamh said, "I ought to go."

Sanden seemed not to hear her, "All I wanted was for my daughter to be safe. No man would have done any different from me." He stopped. When she didn't answer him, an obscene grin formed upon Sanden's face. He pursed his lips, made a little sucking sound with them.

Niamh remembered the night before. The way he'd come

to her, placed his mouth in front of hers. How much stronger he'd been afterwards.

"Don't you dare," she growled.

"Or what?"

Niamh was looking around the room. For what, she didn't know. For garlic, for a crucifix, for a silver gun with silver bullets. There had to be something. Her eyes settled on the coal scuttle. It had been deposited by the grate. She could wield it like a metal club, strike him on the head. She'd knock him down, treat him the same way he'd treated Jenny.

She walked to the fireplace.

Sanden said, "What were those women? So withered, so wild in their attire."

Niam lifted the scuttle. "And what sort of thing are you?"

"The prisoner of your friend, of the curse she cast on me. People assume that it is a blessing to live as I do. You think that, with so much time at my disposal, I must have done something extraordinary. But thirteen generations of my descendants have been born inside these walls, and I have not been free to walk more than half a mile beyond them. Can you imagine how bored I am of dales, of meadows, of the grievances of the little people?"

The scuttle was still in her hand. "You want me to pity you?"

"No. Think of the days I have in front of me – I shall ride through the city, a power beyond resistance. Your monarch will set garlands on my head."

Niamh felt herself burst with fatigue, with rage, with the determination to be somehow revenged on this monster.

She lifted the scuttle again, felt his eyes upon her.

She said, "Tell me about your descendant, Hector."

"What do you know of him?"

"That he lived in London. And died there, six weeks ago."

Edward paused before answering, "He was the bravest, the best of my family. He passed young, a heart attack. It was a bitter tragedy to my kin."

Niamh put down the scuttle. She said, "It was Jenny who killed him. He was in so much pain, he wept. His child beside him."

The look of hatred on Sanden's wrinkled face – it matched the misery of the morning, the pain in her body as she thought of Jenny.

"Go, minx," he said.

"There's something I wanted to ask you," Niamh said. "Something my companion told me. She said the two of you had been friends, more than friends in fact. In your eyes, she said, she'd been a temptation and she resisted you. Was that what the trial was about?"

"I never touched her."

The fury on Sanden face - it wasn't the revenge she'd needed. But it was something. A victory enough, and one she could draw on later.

"Leave," he said, "before I do something you regret."

"Happy to," she told him.

Niamh would have gone right away, walked to the village, taken the bus to London. But she couldn't, not yet – there was somewhere else she needed to be first. For it was Monday morning, the weekend was over, and she had unfinished business in the village. The assize was still sitting, the jurors hadn't reached their verdict. Niamh made her way to the inn, to the hall. The people of the village were there again, sitting in their obedient ranks.

"Gentleman of the Jury," the landlord was saying as she took her place in the hall. "It is your duty to get rid of any thought that might inflame your minds, whether it's about the defendants or the crime they're accused of – despicable as it is to all God-fearing folks."

He summarised the facts they'd been told.

As the landlord went on, Niamh let the words swirl around her head. She could imagine the scene now, see it in her mind's eye. She saw Edward Sanden's daughter, how young the girl had been, not tall enough to reach her mother's waist. She was wearing a black dress, not so different from Jenny's. Over it, a white apron had been wound. The girl reached for the hound, went to pet it. The dog growled. Deep, from within its chest, a sound came like broke glass. It came closer, barked again. Anne drew back. She saw on the lips of the creature's mouth, white flecks of foam. An old man was standing in the girl's kitchen. His shirt was torn at the shoulder. The left side of his face was caked in old, dried, blood. He did not breathe. Niamh could see the fear in the young girl's eye. She stood there, shivering.

Closer the old man came, his cold hand reaching out to touch her. Her mother rushed to Anne's side. Held her, hugged her, did everything she could to calm her weeping, howling, child. *What is it, my love, what hast thou seen?*

The landlord said, "In December, Margaret Waite came to the house, carrying a baby wrapped up in cloth. Margaret Waite told Anne Sanden that the baby would take her life, that it would suck out 'er blood. Or so the witness claimed."

Niamh swallowed, forced the visions away.

At noon, the jury left. Within the hour, they had returned. Had they reached a verdict? They had. The room silenced. "Not guilty," the foreman said.

Even as he spoke those words, Sanden was on his feet. "How dare you!" He appealed to the crowd. "You know what these women did; you cannot leave their crimes unpunished."

Niamh looked at the people around her. They woke.

They looked at Sanden, their eyes rich with scorn. "You fool," one said. She remembered two days before, the chase. She'd walked with the people then, seen them as automata in the Sandens' service. It had seemed to her that the people were trapped in the past, trapped in a state of loyalty to their masters. But they weren't at all. She'd forced together two things which needed to be distinguished: the weight with which the past dominated the village – and the opinions of an older time. The original Chorley folk had been independent-minded, iconoclasts. They'd listened to the gentlemen and chosen to ignore them. As their descendants rose, told Sanden to be quiet she saw them in a new light. They, too, were no-one's catspaw.

"For God's sake–"

Out the villagers went. "Enough," they said.

An old fool, a zealot, one juror called him.

"I will not forget this insult. I will remove myself the source of the evil–"

She almost felt pity for Sanden, ranting at the people as they deserted him.

Niamh found a route away. The two miles to St. Andrews Church, main roads the whole way. It was a piece of foolishness on her part, keeping to the main roads, avoiding the footpaths and bridleways which had been her companion the past few days, but she wanted to feel the comfort of cars, of electric lights. She needed to be back in the twenty-first century.

A left turn led her to St. Andrews. There was a dry-stone wall in front of it. In the churchyard stood a yew tree, ancient and sagging, its trunk gnarled and hollow, twisting like something liquid. The church itself had thick stone walls and wooden pews. The nave was dark, gloomy. The pews, though, were magnificent. At the back, a seat had been carved in mahogany, built into the walls of the church. It was raised above the rest of the building, even above the priest. The throne was padded, cushioned, and reserved for the Sanden family, of course.

Niamh went outside. She saw an altar tomb, raised, and marked in white stone. Niamh sat on the park bench beside it, read an inscription list of Sandens with the dates of their births and deaths. Edward's name was there, and the same date of burial that she'd seen online, 1643. Not that she believed it. His descendants had been the aristocracy of this village kingdom, its merchants, priests, and teachers. She wondered why Edward came here. Whatever he'd told Isidore, she very much doubted that he'd come here to count the distant generations of Sanden dead. She stood, found the strength to walk on a little further from the road. At the end of the graveyard were lesser stones, worn down by the sun and the rain. Niamh walked to a group of three stones, stood to the side of them. This was the place to which Sanden came.

Niamh found the last grave in the yard. There was a stone, grey, with spots of lichen on it, and in all senses unremarkable save for this: into the flat gravestone an iron cross had been driven. It had split the stone. The metal pole stood three feet tall above the ground with a similar length of iron no doubt below, piercing the wooden box beneath, pinning its occupants, to prevent them from emerging, escaping to unexpected life. Seeing it, Niamh's feet stumbled beneath her. She'd read of witches' graves in her history books, and the steps people took to protect themselves against the dead. But these women had been vindicated. What she was seeing wasn't peasant superstition, nor the weakness of ordinary country people, it was Sanden's determination – his wealth – his shame and his demand for vengeance.

She bent down to read the stone, saw the two rows of

nine teeth, and beneath them a carved time-glass. It read, "HERE LIES Ye BODY OF / MARGARET WAITE WIFE TO / ISAAC. DIED AGED 46 / YEARS DEC.d June / 23rd 1613. / Here lies Jennifer / Gill aged 35 years / and of their friend / Mary aged 9 years / DIED June 23rd, 1613. / Suffer little children and forbid them not to come unto me."

June 23rd. Four hundred years ago tomorrow. The day the assize had ended. It took Niamh a moment to process what she was saying. The women had been acquitted. They weren't hanged. If they'd been killed, then it wasn't the state. It had to be Edward. Their relatives had paid for their gravestone. Sanden wouldn't accept his defeat, he'd staked their graves. "I'm so sorry," Niamh whispered. "You won, and he couldn't forgive you." She slumped to the ground, struck a weak first at the earth beneath her.

That evening, she was back in Sanden Hall. Niamh was tired – too tired to think. Her room was quiet. Someone had come in the daytime and left the chamber in a state of superficial order. New sheets had been put on the bed. A white wooden chest had been moved to obscure the parts of the walls from which no amount of washing had removed the pink stain. Niamh left the furniture where it was. She sat at the dressing table, with its glass top, making a mental inventory of her resources. She had the empty tankard, which had once held several fingers of London water, her iPod, the keys to Vron's place, her train ticket home.

If Jenny had been here, she would have urged Niamh to search for Sanden in the house, find his room. She should confront him now, stab him in the heart. But with what weapon? Niamh didn't even know where he slept.

She was thinking to herself it needed to be done at nighttime. As she thought the words, she hated them, but it was the one answer. Attack Sanden in the daytime, and Mrs Armstrong would see them, Wallis too. It had to be done at night.

Round and round her thoughts circled without resolution.

There were friends of Jenny's, in London. She had other companions, Niamh knew, Mirelle Jones, others too, but Niamh did not know their names, had no way of summoning them. Time was running out. Another night she could explain. A second would be impossible. She imagined Jenny telling her, *Tonight, it is your one chance.* But how?

Her body was crying out for sleep.

While Niamh still had no one to help her, no weapon, no plan–

One small idea, at least, did occur to her. Following it, Niamh inched through the house. She opened the bolts of the back door, went out into the darkness. Her mind aching with tiredness, she stripped down to her underclothes. Then, into the inky darkness she waded. Over stones covered in water slime, through mud. Down she went into the reservoir, until it was deep enough to float. She lay on her back, taking each breath slow. She waited there. She took pleasure in the sense that she could lie there without sinking, her body buoyant within the water.

It seemed to her the most basic thing to do, to swim. Isn't that how everyone lives, in the days before we're born; isn't that how everyone lives in the womb, the safest place of all? We swim – we are content in that home of shadows. We grow, our world narrows. A moment of change is coming upon us, we can feel it. The chance of discovery – the brightness of the light outside – it fills us with joy. In that revolution essential to our being, we feel ecstasy and we are wretched. Both. We want the extraordinary novelty of the outside world. With no less passion, do we fear the change which will tear us from our home.

Niamh sucked the damp air deep into her lungs. She needed to transform, find the strength to defeat Sanden. She had to become the very incarnation of revenge – take on the role which Jenny had always urged on her, and which she had always refused.

She thought, *Life begins with a breath.*

She stared at the sky, saw the half dozen lights which could have been stars or might have been satellites. She let the water lap at her. She felt the stillness inside its depths, its subtle currents. She gave a desultory kick, hoping to take herself away from the house – but not too far. She felt the liquid returning her, leading her back to the point of her beginning.

Niamh remembered the ease with which Jenny had swum, with mighty kicks from her strong legs. The memory of her friend caused her face to grimace. She found, to her delight, comfort in the dampness. All day, her mind had been useless, her senses dull, her reactions slow. The water stung her back to life.

She turned onto her front, made as if to copy Jenny. She would be strong in liquid, at ease there. She let her shoulders sink beneath the surface. Then, with a great kick, she swam through the darkness. She let the air escape from her lungs, bubble unwanted to the surface. Further down into the darkness, she reached–

CHAPTER 16
WATER ALWAYS GETS IN

It was one in the morning and Niamh was back in her room. She felt many of the same sensations as the night before – which was cool as the temperature dropped, then she was on edge as if she could hear something moving at a distance but within the house. She rose. If it was Sanden's intention to surprise her, as he'd done the night before, very well, she'd outwit him. The floorboards sagged beneath her bare feet. She inched forwards. She felt tired, anxious. She told herself that she was not alone – that she had Jenny as a memory to inspire her. Black shapes loomed at her in the darkness. She heard the same scraping sound. In the distance, a heavy box was being dragged over a wooden floor. All her things, she collected. The train ticket, het phone. Into her bag and onto her back they went. Through an empty bedroom she walked. She found herself standing by what ought to have been a door. She pushed at the wall, felt the cool, soft dampness of plaster. Beyond the wall – that's where the movement was coming from. Niamh's ears pricked, the hairs at the back of her neck stood tall. Her throat tightened. There was something behind that barrier. Something hidden, something moving. She could hear it breathe, listen to her. She shivered.

From the far side of the wall came the same scraping again. It was louder than ever. It must be there – it was there, but how to get through? She searched the plaster with her hands. There had to be a doorway hidden there. She found nothing.

Niamh scrabbled at the wall, reached out with her fist, punched it in to the plaster. She shouted out in pain. She released dust, debris. No way through.

An answer dawned on her. She raced back to the main corridor, down a first flight of stairs, down a second. The way led to the empty dining room, to the main hall, and the main entrance. Inside the front doorway, she stood catching her breath.

From here, she could walk to the other side of the house, the one which held Mrs Armstrong's room, and not her room alone, but all the other Sanden dwellings. The place that the sound had been coming from was where the two sides of the building met. There, at the house's heart, that's where the old man was.

To the kitchen she ran next, looking for the wooden block in which the knives had been. She couldn't see it. There was no time.

Looking from place to place she saw – the pin from Mrs Armstrong's ascot hat abandoned on the table. Iron to defeat a monster. It sat heavy in her hand, the odds were hopeless. But there was no better weapon offering itself in the gloom.

Unwilling to waste another second, Niamh ran to the stairs. Up them she went, up a second staircase. Until she was on the same floor as her bedroom, at the furthest side of the building. The passage was dark. It smelled of earth dug from a swamp, of mould, of suffering. She came to a corner. Niamh was breathing hard, her heart leaping inside her chest. As she turned, she found a door – pulled it open.

She reached for the light. "Got you."

This was, as she'd predicted, Sanden's own room – but it was bare. No, not bare. Niamh blinked for a moment, waited for her eyes to adjust. On the white plaster walls were drawings, done in ink and pencil. They were like the pictures she had seen in Edward's commonplace book. Drawings of soldiers ordered here and there. Stickmen fighting their battles. In the book, there had been no more than a single page of sketches, a dozen fighters that was all. On the wall of Sanden's room there were more of the soldiers. Dozens of them, with sashes on their backs, aiming their muskets. Hundreds of them, drawn in jackets and breeches. While even greater numbers fled from them, their waists bare, feathers on their heads. The dead victims of empire. The natives whose fear lay, she supposed, in every propertied heart at that time. When a red man danced, a white European saw his own brutality reflected at him. Drawing lay upon drawing, a fascination with conquest and killing. She wondered how long Sanden had lain in his room, how often he had risen in fury to draw the figures which occupied his dreams. And where had these images come from – what vile rumours had fed them?

The furniture consisted of a chair, an oak case, and a chest. At the front of the case, which was four feet tall, and six feet wide, were a small set of curtains. Opening them, making as little noise as she could, she saw they held a bed of sorts. Edward's, she was certain of it.

In front of the bed, she found an open wooden box. It was as long as a coffin but narrower, a foot deep, and a foot wide. His sword-chest; it was empty. That must be the source of the dragging sounds she'd heard.

"Where is he?" Niamh said. She closed her eyes, listened for a sound that didn't come. He'd gone outside, hadn't he?

She switched the light off. *Quiet*, she told herself.

Back she traced her steps, slower this time. Walking with care, taking every effort to ensure that the remaining inhabitants of the house could not hear her. Back she went, until she was in the main hallway, by the great oak door, which was closed but not locked. Niamh went through, and then she was on the path which led down to the reservoir. Gravel beneath her shoes, a full moon in the cloudless sky. She needed to think – where was he heading?

He still had unfinished business. Niamh was sure of it.

But where? And then, she remembered – the accused women. Four hundred years ago to the evening, their murders recorded on the gravestone.

"You've gone to Jenny's home, haven't you?"

Out into the dark Niamh ran – except it wasn't dark at all. The sky was clear, the moon full and the light from it so strong that, if Niamh had wanted, she might have read a book by it. She left the house behind. To her left side was the great expanse of water beyond Sanden Hall. In front of her stretched the path which led by the lakeside. She ran. Past trees and bushes, she raced. Between elms and willows, she dodged.

She remembered her first day in Chorley – it couldn't have been more three days before, and yet it felt three lifetimes ago. She'd been looking for the path that joined Jenny's home and Sanden Hall, and she hadn't found it. Now Niamh understood why. The path was there, there was gaps enough through which you might have ridden a horse if you were so inclined. But the fight of it was sheltered by the trees from the lake's far side.

It was too far. Her legs were stiff as iron but still she ran. She breathed the cool, damp, air deep into her lungs. She was running for the sake of Jenny, for the other women too. She was charging along the path to stop a crime, if by any chance Niamh could. She was rushing in the hope that she could defeat him. The night before, Sanden had killed her friend. Tonight, she would frustrate his plans, prevent a murder – or its re-enactment. Even as Niamh raced, fear beating in her heart, a sound came to her from the distance, the splash of something heavy stepping into water. Niamh tried to estimate how far ahead of her Sanden was.

Fifty metres, she reckoned. She wasn't going to make it in time.

Niamh kept on running. She was on the footpath which led beside the reservoir. The path took a sharp left, stopped by the waterside.

In front of Niamh lay a vast expanse of open water. The moon was bright above it. She saw Sanden, striding in slow, relentless steps through the lake. "Stop!" she shouted. He turned and leered at her, his face a flurry of hatred. Then turned back towards his destination. Over a submerged path he hurried, to the ruins where Jenny's house had been.

Edward had reached his destination. It was a rustic cottage, white stone walls, two windows, a grey, glimmering, thing – not an apparition quite, nor something real, but the past and the present overlain upon each other like drawings upon drawings.

He lifted his fist and beat upon the door.

Three people walked out, stood in front of the building, bowed their heads at Standen, the poet, the gentleman, their social superior. The first was an older woman wearing the same peasant clothes Niamh had seen the day before. The second was a younger woman, dressed in dark shapeless clothes. The third was Jenny. Jennifer Gill. Tonight, she was a spectral apparition in her black dress. It sparkled in the moonlight.

The antique and the modern lay upon themselves, the present and the historic, two moments bonded together by the heat of Sanden's fury.

Running into the water, ignoring the damp as it sucked itself into her shoes, made her slip on the clay soil, Niamh urged herself onwards. She kept her eyes on the scene in front of her. Sanden towered over the old woman. Back, he reached with his right hand. Then he thrust his sword forwards, tip-first, piercing her chest. The woman cried out in pain. clawed with her hand at his face. He pushed her backwards, watched her fall.

Next, he turned to face the apparition of a child. She stood quaking as he threw her to the ground. He held his sword in two hands and thrust down with it. Down, he stabbed again, a fearful smile upon his eyes. His blade pierced the girl's grey nightgown. His actions were slow, careful – had his victims fought then they could have escaped him. But they stood where they were, made immobile by fear.

The girl cried out in pain.

Niamh could hear Edward's breathing, it was weak. Whatever magic he'd worked on her the night before, it had changed little - he was not a well man.

She raced onwards, stepping deeper into the water, trying with every desperate breath to put herself beside Sanden, to stop the last of the murders.

She could do it, she had to.

Reaching for Jenny, the third of the shades, Edward pulled her to a kneeling position. He dragged his sword along the nape of her neck. Blood spattered outwards, dripped on the reservoir. "Thou, villainous wench," he whispered, "Satan's own fondling; from this safe place you must leave. Not on earth, not in the firmament shalt thou find a place of peace. Go as far as Satan will take you. Flee – *I command it.*"

There was a dreadful sound – a wail, interrupted mid-scream.

Niamh peered at the dark water, saw no sign of Jenny.

Sanden turned to face her, pointed his sword at her as he had at Jenny. "You thought you would follow me," he said. "Very well, you've seen it all. And now I am done. I am free,

I can go anywhere I like. I will have such fun as you could not imagine."

"You'll have to get past me."

"You? When I have removed from this world a source of malice."

"You killed three innocent women."

"Don't pretend you could stop me."

Niamh took a step back.

He strode with long, patient, steps through the water, his wrinkled face smiling, making him seem as eager as a young man on a first date. He lifted his sword again, pointed its tip towards her. "Why shouldn't I do to you what I have done already to your friend?"

"You want me to beg for my life?"

"I offer you a choice. Resolve me the truth. Admit she was a witch, which she must have been, for how else could she have returned to this world, except through the magic of some sympathetic power? If she was not in league with the Devil, then why was I cursed? Tell me she was a sorceress. Admit she brought you here to cause me suffering. Beg for your life, ma1ke it convincing, and I shall find a use for you."

"She's dead. What makes you think you I'd betray her?"

He touched the top his sword to the side of Niamh's neck. He held the cold metal tapped it with a brutal softness against Niamh's burning cheek. "Here is reason enough."

"You want me to lie?"

"Tell me the nature of the creature to which you gave your allegiance."

"Her name was Jenny," Niamh said. "She was accused of witchcraft, but a jury acquitted her. They freed her – and all the women."

"So be it." Higher, he lifted his sword. With two hands he held it up over her head, as if intending to split her skull in two. "Merry, merry shall I be." His blade was at its apex and Niamh knew she was doomed. She steadied her feet beneath the water, felt the ground beneath her shoes. She remembered dancing- How light she'd been on her feet then.

She felt a tightness in her chest. It was the pressure of everything, the sense of life preparing to abandon her. It was the defeat which would happen soon enough.

His arms were descending. She stepped back, twisted sideways. She waited for the metal to connect with her head, to cleave her skull in two. She crouched in the water, a supplicant before her king. The grey hatpin useless in her hand.

She looked up, and saw that he had stopped the sword's descent, held the blade dangling inches above her head. He grinned. He stuck it, tip first into the water. It must have found the earth beneath, as it stood there, its pommel glinting like a cross

She said, "Why didn't you kill me?"

Closer Edward stepped, until he was standing before her. While Niamh remained kneeling in the mud, too tired to resist to him.

Edward placed both hands around her neck. He said, "I have a better plan." His thumbs squeezed on her windpipe. His lips pursed into a greedy circle. His lips came closer-

In that moment, it wasn't Edward speaking, it was them all. It was Liam, gossiping about her behind her back. It was Jake, it was the boys in her class, sharing the graffiti. All the stupid, thoughtless, men. Thinking about what *they* wanted, never her.

She threw herself up, out of the water. With a strength she could not have imagined, she struck upwards with the hatpin.

He took a slow step back.

As he did, she drove the pin up, skewered with it through his ribs and into the soft meat behind them. Onwards Niamh pressed with her weapon, pushing into it with the strength of both her hands. It was not unlike sticking a skewer into a roast to check the meat was done. The juice oozing around the metal. The smell was rank – a foul, black liquid dripped from her blade. The air stank of blood, of bile, of poison.

"They were innocent," she said. "Every one of them."

Then it seemed to Niamh as if someone else was holding the weapon, were twisting it deeper into his heart. She saw him stumble for the first time. She let go. No longer guided by her, the pin was digging deeper into the old man's chest. His body quivered as the metal object dug its way further in.

"All changed," he said.

Into the wound the iron pin went. Invisible hands worked the wound wider. The old man fell to his knees. He let out a great, long, slow breath.

His flesh sagged, became loose. His skin began to sink inwards. Sanden pulled himself up, as if to stand. The wound grew. Flesh sundered, as when a child has been making a sand-castle on a beach. Then, as a last act of defiance against the tide, the girl pours water over her own creation. In the towers tumble, down the fortress falls.

There was a black hole where his chest had been. His neck. His face–

Gone now, gone in its entirety.

Niamh gave one last look around her. There was nothing to see but the lake, the darkness. She remembered Jenny's gravestone, the metal pin which had been hammered into the stone. A pin for Sanden too – she smiled, it was fitting, she supposed.

"Well, fuck you," she said.

After that, she slipped into the water. She sat there for a while, the liquid around her, seeping into her clothes. Niamh wasn't cold. She was thinking about her life and long ago and how things had been with Liam and Jake. Even Aitch. She was thinking about her course, the sheer stupid fact of it, the tutorials she'd missed. There would be a list somewhere. She was thinking about her mother, her sister, about all the life that had been going on the last week, all of it without her, ignoring her. They had been fine without her, would be.

"Edward," a voice was calling, "Edward?" Mrs Armstrong said again.

Niamh raced back to the shore. In the comforting darkness, she hid. The night hung low, as thick as the smell of pines. It had been warm in the water but now she was cold. She would walk to the station.

Within a day, she would be in London, back home. Vron would welcome her, feed her, treat Niamh as well as any prodigal child. All she had to do was avoid the lights from the houses. She would keep away from the road, hide from strangers.

CHAPTER 17
LONDON, AGAIN

Without Jenny, the city seemed busier, dirtier, and less forgiving. Niamh made her way to Vron's maisonette, lay in her bed, mute, and friendless. She'd missed one exam already, had others waiting for her, made no effort at revision. After that, days passed, each longer than the day before. Phone calls from her mum, which she didn't take, the digits fading to darkness.

Niamh walked through the streets, waited at the canal-side. She was listening for some unknown kin, whistling, singing in the distance. Sometimes, it seemed to her that the night itself was talking to her, but she could not understand the words. She lay on the floor, resting there, distrusting the bed's embrace. On the wooden surface beside her lay mugs filled with water, bowls too. She kept a cloth, left it damp on her face as she slumbered.

Niamh could have done with some tenderness from her landlady, but Vron had moved on to better things. Dominic had bought her a smartphone, and Vron loved the apps. There was one for shopping, another which linked you to the people you'd known at school.

"Its's amazing," Vron said, "to think how we're all connected, no-one more than five friends away from anyone else, and before you try to talk to someone, you poke them and when you do they message you back the same day. They must, it's the rules."

Niamh smiled at her, enjoyed her landlady's enthusiasm.

She wanted to join in but the darkness she had seen it has settled deep insider her. "It sounds amazing," she said.

"Ask your mum," Vron said. "She'll get you one too."

"I will," said Niamh, knowing she never would.

Another evening, it was Dominic who took her aside. He waited till Vron had gone upstairs. He sat down facing Niamh on Vron's wooden bench. In a quiet, little voice he said, "Thank you for your advice. You were right, all along."

"About what?"

"Posing the question," he said. "I would have been a fool to ask it, and I've been one of them too often in the past. I've had a good thing going, and I almost ruined it."

"You didn't listen to me, did you? Please tell me you didn't. For God's sake, Dominic," Niamh told him. "Go up there right now and ask her. Show some backbone."

"All right," he said.

The next morning, Vron broke the news – the two lovers were engaged. Niamh laughed, lifted her face into a warm smile. At last, some good news.

But where would she live when they married?

Afterwards, when Vron stood outside Niamh's room, she wasn't sighing at the chaos of her maisonette. She was staring at her phone, catching up with all the people she'd forgotten to tell. There were no more little chats with Niamh, no exchanges of gossip. She didn't call Niamh darling. She didn't speak to her at all. What, anyway, could she have told her landlady, had the two of them spoken? That she'd seen suffering and too much of it? Liam, Jenny, Edward– What Vron's news demanded was life and Niamh was all out of it.

An email came from the department. It was the Salt Professor, and Niamh stirred at the memory of his name. She'd quite forgotten about him. In his polite, cautious, way he'd tried to persuade her to return to the course. "I read your proposal for a dissertation," the Professor had written, "it has the potential to be a first-class piece of work. You are an asset to our department, and I urge you to keep going with it."

In the department they were going to discuss Niamh's case. The Salt Professor would tell the meeting that Niamh was a student of enormous potential. They'd be looking at the grades for her exams: a first, an upper second, another first in the autumn. Three did-not-attends. They'd be sharing the stories, telling each other how Niamh's friend had died, and isn't depression such a terrible thing. But Liam wasn't a friend, he was more than that to her. If the future had followed along the lines she had been promised. If Liam hadn't been so full of himself, they might have had some fun together.

She promised to think before answering.

Niamh composed an answer to the Professor, redrafted it, added italics, underline. She sent it to her electronic wastebin instead.

She didn't need to reread Malone's Chapter XIII – The *Death of Arthur*, she knew it by heart. She whispered the words to herself, *but some people say that Arthur never died* –

The weather was wretched, cold beyond comprehension. Sodden. The walls of her room oozed damp, smelled foul, and yet she couldn't leave.

Niamh rang her sister. She called Yvonne's place in Aberdeen. No one answered. She phoned a second time, left a message. Rang again.

In the end, it was Yvonne who contacted her. "Jesus, sister," Yvonne said. "Are you all right? You've been chasing me like a stalker."

"I'm sorry."

"You can't come up. We don't have a spare bedroom – no

room in the inn."

"I know that."

"Then why did you call?"

"I wanted to hear your voice. You're happy – that's all I ever wanted."

"There's nothing wrong?"

"Yvonne," she said, "These are the best days of my life."

One final task was left to her. Niamh walked again to the canal tunnel that Jenny had used as a home. She brought with her a letter for Mirelle.

Niamh had written that she reckoned that Mirelle must have worked this out for herself, but here she was confirming that Jenny wouldn't be returning. In her message, she apologised. Niamh said that she understood what Jenny had meant to Mirelle. She explained that they'd fought Sanden together. She said she hoped that Mirelle would gain some consolation from the knowledge that Jenny had died on her own terms, resisting an evil she hated.

Niamh walked the last stretch of road, descended towards the tunnel in which Jenny had lived. She was expecting to see the silver hairbrush Niamh had given her. She was planning to leave the brush wherever it rested. She thought she would stare for a while at the canal, at the green pond-weed growing thick in the water, at the things that people had abandoned. Plastic bottles. Cans. She was intending to leave the envelope on Jenny's ledge. She reckoned that Mirelle would find the letter but whether the woman would speak to her, she didn't know.

All these plans were still tumbling through her head as Niamh saw – not an abandoned ledge, but a line of a dozen tents all pitched one next to the other. Mirelle Jones's tent was at the head. On it, words had been posted, "Fear needs to change sides," and besides those words the women's symbol and a cartoon of a knife had been drawn. Niamh paused, thought for a second she had come to the wrong place. She realised, sighing, that she hadn't.

There were two women standing between Mirelle's tent and Jenny's ledge. Tall, their heads shaven as if they had joined an army. Purple for loyalty, green for hope. Above their t-shirts, marks could be seen. Someone had gone with a knife and cut three marks into the flesh above their collar bones, ersatz gills, in honour of Jenny.

Niamh came closer.

"Stop there," the taller of the gilled women said.

"I've come with a message."

"Who for?"

"For Mirelle."

"The sister is not accepting visitors."

"She'll want to see me."

"Val," a voice said. "It's fine."

Mirelle's tent was empty. All you could see were the pink and orange nylon walls from which the structure was made. With the light pouring in, it was like being inside a shrine.

"Come here," Mirelle said. She sat her visitor beside her. She put on glasses to read Niamh's letter. She read the first side. "Dead?" she asked, her nose wrinkling.

"I thought you'd be more surprised."

"She said he was a powerful adversary."

"Jenny seemed pretty invincible to me," said Niamh.

"Then you saw half. You saw the strength of her purpose, but not the price she paid for it." Niamh's face must have quivered at that word, *half*, because Mirelle paused, smiled, looked at her with greater sympathy. "Look, I'm glad you came. We knew to expect the worst. Jenny had never been gone this long before. We knew how much it mattered to her. We were already planning a service of celebration. You should come; the women who've joined us, they'd be glad to meet anyone who knew her."

"She wouldn't have wanted you to make a cult."

"We're not that." Mirelle's face remained wrapped in its customary smile.

"The cuts on the women's necks?"

"They serve a purpose. We need a supply of confident women. There are bad men ou there, they deserve all that's coming to them."

"Bad men, like the villains in a Hollywood film?"

Mirelle put down the letter. "When we talk about violence against women, what we're talking about is real. Men hit us, their blows leave bloodstains behind. Their fists break women's jaws. We see how many of the culprits are men, were taught from childhood to see their strength as the last, unbreakable, power that all men hold over all women. Each of us have felt the consequences of male power. All of us have been left quaking, at one time or another, by the fear of violence. At night, we cannot sleep. We spend our days looking over our shoulders, wondering where the next attack will come from. There are some women, so burdened by what happened to them, that they did not survive. Wouldn't it have been better if they had listened to Jenny's words? Others, too, came close. Until we learned that if we arm ourselves, if we resist, then there is no longer any reason to be afraid."

Mirelle waited for Niamh to contradict her. But Niamh didn't know what she thought, had no enthusiasm for another argument.

Mirelle said, "Come, sister. Are you saying women's resistance is childish?"

"I am all up for strikes and protests. How is the world ever going to improve unless we change it? But – *fear needs to change sides* – it's too much."

Mirelle didn't seem to hear. She sat there, smiling, the self-satisfaction radiating from every pore. Niamh felt sick. The sign on the tent outside – she'd heard what Mirelle had to say but still she hated its bluster. Unlike Mirelle, Niamh had killed a man. It was not a pleasant memory, nor an experience she was planning to advertise.

She said, "You don't need to finish the letter. You can read it when I'm gone." She checked in her pocket for her keys, her phone. She said, "I don't want to fight with you. I don't believe there was anyone who saw more of Jenny than you did."

Mirelle nodded.

"You were the person who taught Jenny London. I saw her a little, but you were with her every day. The man who cursed her, he was a monster."

"Many men have become monsters. Jenny told us–"

Niamh tried to smile but she'd seen that expression on Mirelle's face before. "Spare me the lecture," she said – but in a soft voice.

"Man is what he is. Woman will never be safe from his cruelty until we have met his violence with a power of our own."

"I didn't come here to argue."

"Come, live with us, sister. From what I remember, you weren't happy in your old life. You need a proper home, friends – we can offer you them."

"Join the crusade, kill every violent man, for Jenny's sake? Because there's never any danger, is there, of hitting the wrong target?"

"We have chosen a path, and we shall go where it takes us. We are not blithe to the mistakes people have made, but we do believe that–"

"Things need to change," Niamh answered. "You've said

that already. But who's going to clear up the blood afterwards – or are you leaving that to other women?"

Niamh needed to explain it, for her own sake at least, but the right words wouldn't come. She looked at Mirelle, saw her beatific smile and hated her. Niamh felt small, foolish. She said, "I was on Westminster bridge, two years ago, a march of women. We didn't call it that, but it was. Because that's how life works, doesn't it? All the women's jobs – teaching, nursing – you need degrees to do them. The government was setting the price so high that no one could afford it. The people who were there – when I close my eyes, I see them again – all those thousands of people, that's what it needs to be. It's got to be more than a few vigilantes running through the darkness. When we marched, we were the majority."

Mirelle shrugged, "I hear these words of yours, sister. But then I look again, and it seems to me that your face betrays you. When I talk of ending male violence, your eyes blossom. You blush. While these other things you talk about, you duck your eyes down. You stare at the floor. They don't move you. I can see your deepest wants and–"

Niamh rose. "I'm leaving."

"You can't leave the past behind."

"Nor will I be imprisoned by it."

"You're blushing, the body doesn't lie."

"All right, I'm blushing. If I do – it's because I've had enough this nonsense. I don't believe in your cult. I'm not going to help you."

A week later, Niamh was woken by a knock upon Vron's front door. It was Aitch, scowling. Niamh readied to protect herself against a fresh barrage of accusations, but, when Aitch spoke, the woman seemed more tired than anything. She was in no mood to attack. In a quiet voice, she asked Niamh, "Are you good to talk?"

"I suppose."

Aitch said, "I'm sorry – I was thinking – I hope I don't come over as needy, but Jake has been giving me hell, and I didn't know who I could ask. I thought of you."

"Go on, then."

"There's something I need to show you, back in the halls."

"I've got an essay to write." Niamh felt her cheek blush.

"Do this for me," Aitch said. "Things have been so bad ever since Liam died, and I shouldn't have shouted at you. I was wrong. I want to make things better."

A thin heat cracked the ice which surrounded Niamh's frozen heart. "All right," she said, and went back to her room for her shoes.

At the top of the landing, Vron was leaving her own room. She started at Niamh's approach. "You're not going out, are you?"

From behind Vron's leggings, Tirzah poked a sad nose.

"I'll be back later," Niamh said. "Do we need anything from the shops?"

Vron said, "It's her again, isn't it?"

"She's got a name – Aitch," said Niamh, feeling a vague sense of generational loyalty and no little frustration with her landlady.

"Are you sure it's safe?" Vron said. "The way she used to talk about you," and then the words seemed to drain out of her. As if she couldn't think evil of anyone, not when her own life was such a joy. She said, "I'm an old fusspot, what do I know?"

Niamh saw the twitch on Vron's lips. Whatever doubt it was – Dominic, she guessed – now wasn't the time to hear it. "I won't be long," she told her landlady. "They're my friends and you've got to forgive when they ask you."

Niamh opened the front door, Tirzah peering out from behind her.

Aitch didn't say much in the bus, she looked out the window. Niamh did the same. London was making itself ready for the autumn – the people busy, their eyes downcast. Everyone in their own bubble. "I missed you," Niamh said. A part of her wanted to explain all the strange things she had seen – Jenny, Sanden. She wanted to but couldn't.

"I missed you too," Aitch said. "All the time."

Niamh followed Aitch to her room. There was Jake, sitting on Aitch's bed. "Hello," he said, and he looked at Niamh – shone her a shy, half-apologetic, smile.

He reached up for Aitch and bent his face down to kiss her. "You're back," he said and bent down and touched his lips to her cheek with such gentleness. Like she was a creature made of paper and if he was too harsh with her, she would break.

Niamh said, "Is this a bad time?"

Aitch smiled. "It's not. *It's not.* We've been planning this for weeks. Did your landlady tell you – we've been coming round every day?"

Jake said, "We've got a present for you–"

"I don't need anything," Niamh told him, recalling the cruelty of their last encounter. She still wasn't sure if she quite trusted him.

"To thank you," he said. "I'm sorry. I shouldn't have pulled that nasty prank."

If the purpose of giving her this apology was to calm the anger simmering inside her, then his words were a failure, and yet – and yet, after the disaster that had befallen Jenny, all Niamh's losses since seemed more modest by comparison. It was good to see Jake and she was in no mood to hoard her grievances. She said, "Do you mean it this time?"

"Cross my heart and hope to die."

She shook her head. “I’m not sure I believe you.”

“Come and see for yourself.”

Jake led her to the lift.

“Aren’t you coming with us?” Niamh asked Aitch.

“I will. Give me a minute,” Aitch said, her voice distracted.

The block in which the students were housed was an ordinary, unremarkable, London building. Ten storeys high. Red from the outside, plated in sheets of plastic. Inside, it was corridor after corridor of student homes, all built to the same specification. Single beds, bathroom sinks. The smell everywhere of sweat and hormones.

Jake stood beside her as the lift rose. “Look at you,” he said, his voice soft. “You’re as much a victim as any of us.” She looked down. He was wearing a pair of black Oxfords. They were so terribly well-polished, as if he’d poured liquid wax over them.

The lift stopped at the ninth storey. After that, there were stairs which led you to the tenth. Here stood the last four rooms. The corridor was silent.

Niamh was struggling to understand why he’d brought her here, but on looking around the tenth floor, she understood at last. The other occupants must have left for the holidays. In their absence, the managers of the building had done something Niamh hadn’t seen before, they’d unlocked the hatch in the roof, let down the ladder which led upwards.

“You see,” Jake said. “It’s my way of saying sorry.”

Niamh followed him up the ladder.

She found herself on a balcony with a view. The white tower of Senate House. Trees, office blocks. In the distance, the rich men’s playthings of the City.

Jake stood behind her. His arms on her shoulders. “Isn’t it great?”

"It is," Niamh told him, even though heights had always made her wobble.

"It's ours," he said. "The best view in London."

She said, "Everyone forgets how the city depends on the river."

He didn't seem to hear her. "The best," he said again, shoving at her waist.

After that, Niamh was no longer on the platform. She was in the air. Above her, Jake was shouting, broken sounds came to her, Liam's name, Helen. He said other things too, although Niamh couldn't hear them. They didn't matter. To him, not to her.

The day rushed at her. It filled her mouth, her clothes. She could have screamed. Did scream, but there was no one to hear her. Nothing but the cold. The damp. Nothing fell with her. Not Jake. She thought of swimming to safety.

If she dived, there might be water to break her fall. But there was nothing to help her. The ground rushed towards her. Ever closer it came. Until at last, it fell upon her, whipping the air from Niamh's lungs.

She asked herself if she was surprised to be falling – she wasn't. Niamh Malone: historian, daughter, road-kill. It seemed a fitting epitaph.

Dying, it turned out, meant the giving away of memories. As she smashed into the ground, as she felt her spine shatter, her heart stop, she was trying to remember the street in Birmingham where she had grown up, the Tesco's at one end, the music shop at the other. The sights of the road were beyond her. She tried to remember her History, the Treaties of Locarno, Rapallo, Brest-Litovsk, but the names slid away, the participants, their consequences. She forgot the names of the cast of Coronation Street. She discarded the memory of the first episode of Eastenders, Lofty and Michelle, the actors' faces familiar from Grange Hill. The shock of the opening credits, of the cartoon drawing of a sausage at head height, a fork attached. Yvonne's last three boyfriends she discarded, the one with the beard. His name began with an F. She had met him, she knew him, she'd laughed at his joke. Now, though, she couldn't recall his face. She couldn't remember anyone's face. She neglected the place where once she'd sat in the pub, listened to Charlize. *It's not you, it's me*. She abandoned the memory of leaving the pub in which they'd drunk, knowing she'd never see her lover again. She could no longer have explained how to walk, how to dress, how to eat. The taste of aloo gobi. How to dance Y-M-C-A. She gave away the French she'd learned in school, *Ma mère, le mer*.

The precious blood ebbed from her brain.

The spill of water across the ground, wasn't that what London had been once, a lagoon, the sweet liquid from the hills mixing with the salt from the sea.

She threw away the blue light of a spring day. The touch of the sun upon her skin. Hills. Rivers. Beaches – her dad's voice. Home already.

Yvonne – how she missed her.

CHAPTER 18
HOME

Niamh rested. She lay in the darkness, days without purpose, time without end, struggling to recall what it was that she had ever –

Known.

What brought Niamh to her senses were sounds, the pop, and fizz of green wood as it burned in the distance. The smell of woodsmoke. She felt the presence of fire near water. Flames. *Danger.* She sensed the threat, flinched from it. Her pulse quickened, the excitement of something new. She smiled. As she lay there in that place between rest and waking, her first move was to her stretch her arms wide. She was going to open her lungs and breathe in the morning air. But then, as she spread her arms, everything was wrong. Her elbows pressed not against bedsheets, rather against something alien which resisted her.

Her arms splashed against something mobile, thick – *liquid*? She was alive, she was in a river, wearing the same jeans and t-shirt in which she'd died.

Not a river, a canal. The banks were straight, man-made. Beyond them stood a field. In the distance, the skeleton of an oak tree. A field. England, it had to be. Her body rolled over and every movement she took made it worse. She kicked, she fought, she tried to right herself, but her face was down, and her feet up. If she opened her lungs, the liquid would drown her no doubt, and this was no empty hillside stream, it was choked with slimy weeds. She kicked at the weeds, broke her leg through the plants.

Someone had summoned her. A woman. Niamh could taste her anger. The unsatisfied rage gave the air a flavour as sweet as treacle. The woman would find Niamh soon. Or Niamh, her. When they met, Niamh would help her. She'd bring succour to the weak, fear to the strong. It was what she did. What all her kind did. Niamh lifted herself up from the dampness. She placed a hand on her neck, felt the flap of skin opening and closing with each breath.

Niamh had needs of her own, too, more urgent than those of the woman who had called her back to life. She could see it all now, feel the paths of her future open before her.

"Jake," she said.

Aitch was in this world somewhere; Niamh was sure of it. But she'd start with Jake.

Afterword

In my story, I lend Jenny Greenteeth to London, the city of my birth and where I have lived most of my adult life. This was a move of some violence, which risks misrepresenting her. In the history of Britain over the last two centuries, Jenny Greenteeth has been consistently a northern legend, with sightings of her recorded in Lancashire and Cheshire and in very few other counties. For many years, parents warned their children against the dangers of stagnant water by saying that the duckweed growing on the surface of ponds, including on abandoned industrial diggings, was the hands and claws of Jenny Greenteeth. Sources speak of a family of water creatures: called variously Jenny Greenteeth, Peg Powler or the Grindylow. Those who want to know more of her history should consult Simon Young's 2019 study, *The Sources for Jenny Greenteeth and Other English Freshwater Fairies.*

In the original myth Jenny's victims are thoughtless boys puffed up by the invulnerability of youth. Put a spirit of female violence in a present-day context and it seemed natural to me that she would be motivated to act in response to different and more contemporary male crimes – controlling behaviour and sexual violence.

My story contains many other matters beyond my take on the Greenteeth; it is as much a memoir of a particular time and of certain relationships, a rethinking of broader issues relating to revolutionary violence, a discourse on resentment and forgiveness. But, in the end, I insist that my Greenteeth is no allegory for anything, nor a mere metaphor. Pull of her mask and she remains Jenny, her enemies are still alive, her path to victory or defeat ever uncertain.

Acknowledgments

I am grateful to the many friends who made this book possible. They include the original readers of my work: Tina Baker, Tansy Hawksley, Jonathan Hannah, Zehra Jamal, Amelia Kyazze, Mahvesh Khan, Remy Maisel, Kathleen Nixon, Scarlett Parker, also Alexandra Hesse, Hayden Scott, Dominic Silvani and Julia Swaby who read various chapters in draft. I am also grateful to those who have mentored me and shaped my writing: Clare Allan, Anthony Cartwright and Jonathan Myerson, Julia Bell and Wes Brown.

I want to thank that core group of friends, who've held me close these past 15 years: Rachel Aldred, Jasmina Cenan, Jake Hotson, Bruce Howard, Adam Di Chiara, Anna Mobbs, Paul Murphy, Matt Saywell, James Woodcock and Leo Zeilig.

I am grateful to the many members of the rs21 writers' group, not least the group's co-convenors Sabrina Huck and Clara Hill, but also Liz Burdon, Hazel Croft, Rachel Eborall, Colin Fancy, Charlie Hore, David Longworth, Ruairidh MacLean and Alexis Wearmouth.

Thanks are owed also to my editors, Sally Orson-Jones and Rebecca Johnson. To the friends who advised me on practicalities including Tina, Tansy and Joel Hames. And, above all, to Anne. Most prosaically, she prepared the covers, the design and the manuscript. Really, her advice, her thoughts and our shared memories inform almost every page of this book. Her love has sustained me through the last 30 years and through the crisis of my last year. Thanks too to Sam and Ben for all their patience.

About the Author

David Renton is a historian and barrister. He has previously published thirty books of non-fiction, including a major study of the contemporary far right, *The New Authoritarians*, and *Never Again,* the history of Rock Against Racism and the Anti-Nazi League in the 1970s. He writes regularly for magazines and newspapers in Britain and the US including the *London Review of Books, The Guardian, rs21 and Tempest.* This is his first novel.